The COLOR *of a* CHRISTMAS MIRACLE

Julianne MacLean

Prologue

I t's Christmas Eve, nearly midnight, and I am on my knees in the snow, praying for a miracle.

To be honest, I have been praying for this miracle every day for the past few years, but never quite like this. This is different. This time, I would really love for things to work out. Not just for my own sake, but for my husband's, because he is the kindest, most generous and compassionate soul I've ever known. He deserves this gift, and I would love for him to receive it.

So I could really use your help.

Let me assure you, I am not asking for a handout. I am not the type of person to feel sorry for myself or expect good things to simply fall into my lap because I prayed for them. To the contrary, I am a realist, and I've learned how to pick myself up and dust myself off when I get knocked down—and I've been knocked down quite a bit in this life. But I've always had faith that everything will work out in the end, exactly as it's meant to—as long as I am willing to do my share and never lose hope.

So I will ask again....

Say a prayer for me tonight. I am a good person, and so is everyone else involved in this. I may not always have felt that way. I might have been angry and judgmental about certain people who caused me pain recently, but the situation has changed.

I have changed.

Although I suppose it would help if you knew what, exactly, you were praying for. Or rather, what I am praying for.

So let me rewind a bit and tell you where I am tonight, and how I came to be here.

Merry Christmas, by the way. I hope all of your dreams come true, and that this is the best Christmas ever. For all of us.

CHAPTER

One

I t's rather remarkable, don't you think, that so many of us can enter adulthood believing that most roads ahead will be straightforward, and that we will step onto a straight path in pursuit of our dreams, and everything will go according to plan.

I don't know why in the world I embraced this idea, considering the fact that I'd been thrown some curveballs in my childhood—curveballs that resulted in heartbreak and loss. Maybe I believed that—because I'd already suffered so much disappointment in my younger years—the odds would be in my favor moving forward.

Or maybe I was able to cling to this surprising sense of optimism because my childhood hadn't *always* been difficult. The early formative years had, in fact, been rather wonderful. For the first twelve years of my life, my younger sister Bev and I were fortunate enough to have been blessed with a loving family—which included two responsible parents who adored us and taught us how to be good people, how to always be considerate of others and place value on family and community. They treated us like angels, and we were as close as any family could be. Our cozy little home in a small, friendly town in rural Nova Scotia was a happy one, full of laughter and love. Bev and I never wanted for anything.

But then it all came crashing down one day when I was twelve and my father went outside to trim the hedge while Bev and I played in the sprinkler. He slipped and fell into the ditch and impaled himself on the clippers. My mother called an ambulance, but my father died before he reached the hospital. He was only thirty-six.

We were all traumatized and devastated, especially my mother who had called him her 'knight in shining armor.' They had been together since the eighth grade and he was the only man she had ever loved.

Suddenly, she was alone without the love of her life to help her raise her two grief-stricken daughters. That first year was full of pain, anger and tears, and over the next few years, we struggled financially. My mother—who had never worked a day in her life—took a waitressing job to support us. Sadly, it wasn't enough to get by on and we eventually sold our cozy little home in a tree-lined neighborhood and moved to a less desirable part of town. Life was never quite the same after that.

Though my mother strove to be strong for Bev and me, I knew how broken she was on the inside. My father's death left a gaping hole in her heart, and she was dismayed by the loss of him.

Sometimes she cried in her bedroom at night when she thought Bev and I were asleep. Whenever I heard her sorrow, I tiptoed to her room and crawled into bed with her, and held her close to comfort her. Bev would come in, too, and we would comfort each other.

I had loved my father with all my heart and soul. He

taught me how to ride a bicycle, how to swim, how to build a campfire, and all the other things fathers do for their daughters—which I didn't appreciate nearly enough when he was alive. I was simply too young to contemplate the possibility that he might be taken from me, violently and without warning.

Later, I looked back on happier times and visualized him as a magnificent shooting star, blazing across the sky before disappearing in a sudden flash.

Sometimes, it was difficult not to be overcome by my anger for having been robbed of such a wonderful man. He would never walk me down the aisle, or be the proud, smiling face in the audience, cheering and clapping as I received my high school diploma.

Whenever I wanted to lash out at God for such cruelty and unfairness, I shut my eyes and struggled to feel gratitude instead for the special years I'd had with my dad—and for the depth of his love for me. I held his love tightly inside my heart.

I never truly got over the loss of him, and that loss has affected how I have lived my life—in good ways and in bad. You will see exactly how, in the pages that follow.

After high school, I was fortunate enough to attend university with the help of academic scholarships and student loans, and I forged ahead with optimism, forcing myself to believe that everything would go my way as long as I worked hard, got good grades, and clung to my integrity on a personal level—because those were the lessons my father had taught me. He was an honorable man with a strong moral compass, and I never stopped believing that he was watching over me, urging me to be the principled young woman he had raised me to be. I didn't want to disappoint him, so I made every effort to be the best person I could be.

I enjoyed good relationships with my professors; I maintained close friendships with the girls in my dorm (they called me their mother hen, because I was usually the one to make sure everyone got home safely from parties).

At the end of four years, I graduated with a Bachelor of Science degree with a major in mathematics. My mother was proud of me for being so "accomplished."

Perhaps I was, on many levels, but I had never fallen in love. I'd never experienced the kind of "head over heels" passion that makes a woman throw all caution to the wind, and that caused me to worry that I was somehow deficient or incapable of intimacy with a man. Perhaps, because of the loss of my father, I possessed a classic fear of abandonment that would haunt me for the rest of my days.

At least, having excelled academically, I was able to achieve personal fulfillment through other means. I went on to earn a degree in education, graduated at the top of my class, and at the age of twenty-four, I was hired to teach math in a top-rated, private elementary school in Halifax with small class sizes. It was located in a renovated Victorian mansion in an upper-class neighborhood in the South End, not far from the entrance to the magnificent Point Pleasant Park, which boasted groomed walking trails and outdoor summer performances by *Shakespeare by the Sea*. Most of the children came from good families and wore smart uniforms with navy blazers and plaid kilts for the girls, grey trousers for the boys.

It was a dream come true for me to land a full-time job

like that straight out of university, doing exactly what I wanted to do: teach and connect with the children. Especially those who struggled in some way personally, as I had struggled after the loss of my father.

During my first year of teaching, I was as happy as anyone could be, although there was still something missing, and I knew exactly what it was.

I wanted love. A family of my own. I didn't want to fear the rug getting pulled out from under me, unexpectedly. I wanted to believe that I had paid enough dues when it came to loss, and the odds for happiness and success would be in my favor going forward.

I prayed that one day, I would be brave enough to open the door when love came knocking. It was almost comical that I didn't hear the sound of the knuckles rapping when it actually happened.

L et me go back a bit, to explain.

On the first day of school at my new job, I had met a young man named Wes Radcliffe. He taught gym and had been working at the school for two years before I arrived. Like me, he was hired straight out of a local university.

We quickly discovered that we lived in the same apartment building, which was not far from the school, so we started walking back and forth together every day.

Our conversations were open and lively. Often we talked about our experiences and challenges as teachers. We shared funny stories and gave each other advice and support when needed.

On top of that, we had all sorts of things in common outside of work, like favorite movies and music. Soon we began spending time together as friends on weekends. But at the end of the school year, when he told me that a woman from his gym had asked him out on a date, I finally realized that I was in love with him—the elusive head over heels kind of love that I'd never imagined I would ever allow myself to feel.

Suddenly, the idea of my best friend going out on a date with another woman sent me into a jealous tizzy. As we rode the elevator in our building, going up, he turned to me and asked, point blank, if he should say yes to her.

My stomach churned with anxiety and I couldn't look at him. All I could do was shrug and say, "If that's what you want to do."

The elevator doors opened, and before I realized what was happening, Wes reached for my hand, pulled me back in, and kissed me passionately on the mouth. The doors shut again and we rode the rest of the way up to his apartment while I lost my mind to happiness and desire, and melted in his arms.

That was the moment I knew that I would be his forever. Body and soul.

I'm not sure what exactly had caused me to throw caution to the wind so completely in the space of a single heartbeat. But looking back on it, it hadn't actually happened in a heartbeat. The strength of our friendship had evolved slowly, building trust and affection one day at a time, walking back and forth from school, talking to each other about personal things without any pressure to date or kiss or flirt.

I had confided in Wes about my father's death early on, and explained how it affected me—how that was probably the reason I'd never been in love. I believe that's why Wes handled me with kid gloves during the first year. He didn't rush me into anything, until that day on the elevator, but by then, we had already built the trust.

Wes, in turn, told me that he was blessed with two parents who were still together and in love after thirty years of marriage. He explained this to show me that happy endings *were* possible, and not every love story had to end in heartbreak. Not every parent is taken away from every child.

When he finally kissed me, I realized he was right—that sometimes love could last forever.

So I accepted the fact that I couldn't live without him. How could I, when he'd become my best friend? (And he was wildly handsome as well; I couldn't take my eyes off him whenever he walked into a room.)

Our blossoming romance was tricky at first, professionally. We both felt a need to keep it secret at work for as long as possible, but eventually—when there was no question that we were serious—we announced it to our co-workers.

Two years later, we tied the knot during the month of October in a cozy church wedding, just outside the city.

Bev was my maid of honor, and as my mother walked me down the aisle, I had a hard time holding back tears because I wished my father could have been there, too. But soon, my tears became tears of joy when I saw Wes looking at me with love and adoration, as if I were the perfect woman he'd always dreamed of marrying.

In his eyes, I saw anticipation for the future, and his expression caused a flood of emotion in me. He was the only man I had ever loved. The only man I trusted enough to keep my heart safe, and I couldn't wait to begin our new life together.

We honeymooned on the Mediterranean—a gift from Wes's parents, who were very well-to-do.

When we returned, we moved into his apartment, which was larger than mine and had better views of the water in the Northwest Arm. We enjoyed sitting out on our balcony in the evenings, watching the sailboats come and go from the yacht clubs.

Those early years as newlyweds were magical, and for the first time in my life, everything seemed to be falling into place, and the hole in my heart was beginning to heal. I wasn't afraid anymore. I was confident that I had made the right decision, taking a fearless leap of faith into marriage and complete, uninhibited love, come what may.

"So what's up?" my sister Bev asked as she got out of her car and found me sitting on one of the benches at the park entrance. It was mid-August, only two weeks before the first day of school, and she and I had agreed to meet and take her dog Leo for a walk. "You said you didn't want to tell me over the phone."

I stood up and approached. "I have some exciting news."

Bev opened the back door of her SUV and leaned in to hook the leash on Leo's collar, then she stood back while he jumped out. Eager to say hello, Leo—a five-year-old golden retriever that Bev had rescued from the SPCA—dragged my petite blond sister across the parking lot toward me.

"Hey, Leo." I rubbed him behind both ears. "It's good to see you, too."

The three of us started off and entered the park where the tree-lined path was wide and shady, with plenty of other walkers, bikers and runners passing us in both directions.

"So…" Bev said, "don't keep me in suspense. Tell me."

I paused, just for effect, and smiled at her. "We bought a house."

Bev stopped in her tracks. Her eyebrows lifted with excitement. "No way! That's great! Where is it?"

I pointed in the direction of the parking lot and beyond. "It's not far from here, on the most adorable little street off of Inglis, close to Saint Mary's."

"That's amazing!"

"I know, right? We're so excited. I can't believe we got it. It has hardwood floors throughout, and three bedrooms. The kitchen and bathrooms need some work, but that's why we got it at such a good price. We can drive by it later, if you like."

"Of course!" Bev hugged me. "Congratulations. This is so great!"

We started walking again, with Leo pulling hard on the leash, hurrying us along.

"So does this mean what I think it means?" Bev gave me a sidelong look.

My sister knew me too well. She understood that neither Wes nor I had wanted to start a family in the high rise apartment building where we currently lived, which was why I had suggested we start shopping for a house sooner, rather than later, because I was turning twenty-seven soon. Not that the clock was *really* ticking, but Wes and I had talked about it, and we were both eager to start a family before either of us turned thirty.

As far as the house went, we wanted something with a backyard and with other young families in the neighborhood, so that our children would have playmates. We weren't opposed to buying a fixer-upper if it meant we could settle down in the South End—the priciest location on the peninsula—but we wanted to be near the school where we both worked and where our children would eventually attend.

I linked my arm though Bev's. "As a matter of fact, it does mean what you're thinking. I guess I can let the cat out of the bag now. We've started trying."

Bev rested her head on my shoulder. "I'm so happy for you. And I can't wait to be an auntie. You know how I love babies."

Bev, who recently completed a nursing degree, had been assigned to the obstetrics floor at the hospital where she worked.

"I'll come and babysit for you anytime," she added, jumping ahead and jogging a few steps when Leo pulled on the leash. "Seriously, this is the best news ever. Does Mom know yet?" she called over her shoulder.

I hurried to catch up. "No, and let's keep it quiet for now. I only just went off the pill, and with the house purchase... We'll be busy for the next few weeks because it's a tight closing. We move in a month. And I don't want to get Mom's hopes up until there's actually some good news to report. It might take us a while."

We passed a lady with two Schnauzers, and they stopped to sniff Leo. We all chatted for a moment, then started off again and turned up the path toward the stone Martello Tower.

"So, was Wes keen to start trying?" Bev asked. "You didn't have to talk him into it? Some husbands are like that, you know. They have to be dragged kicking and screaming into parenthood."

"Not Wes," I replied, as we strode up the hill. "You know he's an only child, and he always felt like there was a lot of pressure on him to be the best at everything when he was a kid, so he wants at least three, maybe four children. It's the money thing that makes him uneasy. He wants to be sure that we're ready, financially, and I'm still paying off my student loans. That's why he wanted to wait until we had a house, so that we're settled and not throwing money out the window on rent every month."

I paused a few seconds, then decided to tell Bev everything.

"But I *did* have to talk him into asking his parents for some money, for the down payment on the house. We didn't have enough saved, and it's a pricey neighborhood. He thought we should keep looking for something cheaper, but it was so perfect. It's like the house we had when Dad was alive. I just couldn't let it go."

"So his parents helped you out?"

"Yes, thank goodness. But he hated asking. He's just so proud when it comes to money. I think it's partly because his father didn't want him to become a teacher. He wanted him to go to law school or medical school or something impressive, where he'd make a giant salary. And then…not only did he become a teacher, but he married one. They're kind of snobby that way. Wes hates giving his father a reason to say I told you so."

"But his parents like you, right?" Bev asked.

"Oh yes. They've always been great to me, especially his mom. I love Barbara."

"And Wes loves teaching," Bev added. "Surely they want him to be happy."

"Exactly." I waved my hand dismissively through the air. "But it doesn't matter. They gave us the down payment, so we'll take it from here. We'll be able to afford the monthly mortgage payments."

Bev grinned and nudged me in the ribs with her elbow. "And soon you'll have a little bambino, and his parents will be over the moon when they see their first grandbaby.

They'll be tickled pink and happy as clams. Then they won't care that their son didn't become a doctor or a lawyer."

Leo spotted another golden retriever running around off leash on the grass next to the stone tower. His owner threw a Frisbee and the dog leaped into the air to catch it.

Leo bolted, dragging Bev behind him. I laughed and hurried to catch up.

Wes and I had been in the new house for a month when our second anniversary rolled around. He surprised me on a Saturday morning with breakfast in bed, a bouquet of flowers, and a card that suggested I get up and start packing, because we'd be spending the weekend at White Point Beach Resort—an ocean front vacation spot only two hours from the city. I'd never been there before but always dreamed about going.

Wes had booked us a rustic cottage overlooking the ocean, and the first thing we did after we unpacked our bags was head down to the white sand beach. We walked arm in arm while chatting over the thunderous roar of the surf.

That night, surrounded by colorful autumn leaves, we went to the main lodge for a delicious meal in the dining room, then retired to our cottage, where we snuggled on the sofa before a hot, crackling fire.

It was one of the most romantic weekends I'd ever known—perhaps even more romantic than our honeymoon—and I let Wes know that he had chosen the perfect anniversary gift.

"These have been the best two years of my life," I told

him as the waves exploded on the rocks outside our window. "I never imagined I could love anyone like I love you. I didn't think it was possible, not for me."

"Because of what happened with your dad," Wes gently replied as he rubbed my shoulder with the pad of his thumb.

A lump formed in my throat, but I swallowed over it to push it back down. "Yes. It just blindsided all of us. One day he was there, the next day he was gone, and for years I didn't want to set myself up to feel that kind of pain and loss again. But then you came along…"

A log shifted in the grate and sparks flew up the chimney.

Wes was quiet for a long moment. Then at last, he spoke. "That worries me, Claire."

I sat up to look at him. "Why?"

"Because…" He hesitated. "You know I'll never leave you, or do anything to cause you pain, but none of us are immortal. I can't guarantee that something won't happen to me, that I won't die young. I hope it doesn't happen, of course. I'd rather live to be a hundred and I hope I do, but life doesn't always work out the way you want it to. And if it ever did happen that way, I hope you wouldn't give up on love altogether."

I frowned slightly. "I know what you're saying, but don't worry. When you kissed me in the elevator that day, I knew I could never walk away. I decided then and there that sharing my life with you was going to be worth it, even if there was pain down the road. I'm a realist. I know we can't live forever—death comes for all of us—but I can't let it stop me from enjoying what we have today."

Wes cupped my face in his hands and kissed away my

tears. "I love you, more than anything, and I can't wait to have a baby with you. Lots of babies. You're going to be an amazing mom."

I smiled. "And you're going to be an amazing dad."

I snuggled back down into the warmth of his arms. "How many kids do you want?" I asked.

"Four," he replied, without hesitation. "Maybe even five. I want a big, noisy family where there's lots of chaos. Not like what I had."

We talked for a while about what it was like for him as an only child, and he admitted that although his family was wealthy and they gave him everything a child could ask for, it was lonely sometimes.

"I'm on board for five kids," I said with a smile. "I want to give you everything, Wes, in return for what you've given me. And I want a big family too, because I know how fragile and precious life is. I want to live it to the fullest. I want our kids to have lots of brothers and sisters, so they'll always have each other, even after we're gone."

Wes kissed the top of my head. "I wish I could have met your father, because he must have been an incredible man—to bring someone like you into the world."

I smiled. "I wish he could have met you, too. He would have loved you."

Wes pulled me into his arms and held me tight. Then, when the fire died down, we went to bed and made love with passion and tenderness.

I felt surrounded by magic.

⌐⊘

Two weeks later, Wes and I sat across from each other at

the kitchen table in our new house, marking assignments and sharing stories about our day.

Suddenly, I felt a rush of euphoria and couldn't contain it. I looked up and grinned at him.

"I don't want to jinx anything," I said, "but I can't help it. Something feels different."

"What do you mean?" Wes set down his pen.

I took a deep breath and let it out. "I think I might be pregnant."

His eyebrows lifted and he looked at me expectantly. "Really? Are you sure?"

I laughed a little. "No, I'm not sure. I haven't taken a test or anything, but it's like I can feel it." I sat back and laid a hand on my belly. "That weekend at White Point… It was the right time of the month for us to try, and I feel all tingly inside, and so happy. And this morning I gagged while brushing my teeth. That's never happened before. And today at lunch, I had the weirdest craving for a hot dog with relish and mustard. And you know I *hate* hot dogs."

Wes rose from his chair and circled around the table. "Babe…this is incredible." He sank to his knees before me and laid his hand over mine, on top of my belly. "Do you know how much I love you?"

"As much as I love you?"

He wrapped his arms around me and rested his cheek on my stomach. I ran my fingers through his thick, dark hair and felt completely at peace with this wonderful man. I wanted to pinch myself. How could I be this fortunate? This blessed? And would our first child be a boy or a girl?

It didn't matter to me. I would be happy either way. I was never so sure that everything was going to work out.

But three days later, I got my period.

I was saddened by the fact that I wasn't pregnant yet, and felt embarrassed and ridiculous for having believed it was so, and for telling Wes about it with stars in my eyes.

When he came home from the gym that night and I explained that we hadn't been successful, I saw the disappointment in his eyes, but thankfully it didn't linger. He dropped his gym bag at the front door, strode forward, pulled me into his arms and held me close.

"I'm sorry," he whispered in my ear while he rubbed his hand up and down my back. "I know how hopeful you were, but we only just started trying. These things can take time."

"That's not what they tell you in high school," I replied, trying to make light of it, even though I felt melancholy.

He chuckled and stood back. "Well, since you're not pregnant, let's drown our sorrows." He took me by the hand, led me into the kitchen for a big bowl of butterscotch ripple ice cream and a glass of white wine.

That's the kind of guy he was. He always knew exactly the right thing to say and do to make me feel better.

As I dug into my ice cream, I decided that I wouldn't suggest such a thing to Wes again. I wouldn't speculate that I was pregnant until my period was at least seven days late and I'd taken a test. No sense in *both* of us getting our hopes up.

CHAPTER

Four

The holiday season proved to be a challenge after Wes
and I had gotten married, because it was difficult to
divide our time between our two families. Though he
was an only child, he had many aunts, uncles and cousins
who traveled from Ontario to stay at the Radcliffe mansion
for Christmas. It was a massive yearly gathering, and
everyone opened gifts together on Christmas morning.

Meanwhile, my family had always enjoyed a quiet,
intimate supper with just me, Bev and my mom on
Christmas Eve—and now we included Wes. So he and I
scrambled to be in both places on that special night—dinner
at 4:00 at my mom's house, and a second dinner at 8:00 with
Wes's family at their mansion on the shores of St.
Margaret's Bay, where we would spend the night.

We arrived at my mom's house early with a salad and a
bottle of wine, and sat down for a traditional Christmas Eve
turkey dinner with all the trimmings. When my mother tried
to pour me a glass of wine from the bottle we had brought,
I politely declined and opted for apple cider instead, which
caused my mother to stare at me curiously for a moment,
and then smile.

Later, Bev took hold of my arm and pulled me into the bathroom.

"What's going on?" she asked while sucking on a candy cane. "Why are you not drinking wine?"

I shook my head and gestured for her to stay calm. "Really. It's nothing. I don't know anything for sure yet. But I'm three days late."

Her face lit up. "Really? Do you think this is it?"

I shrugged. "I don't know. I thought I was pregnant after White Point, but you know what happened there, so I've learned not to assume anything until I take an actual test from the drug store and get a positive result. But I'm really hopeful. Our timing was bang on this month, if you know what I mean."

Bev laughed. "I have a good feeling, Claire. Wouldn't it be the best Christmas present ever? To find out that you're expecting a baby?"

"It would." My body tingled with excitement.

The following morning, at the Radcliffes', pandemonium broke out when fourteen of us, all in our pajamas, gathered around the Christmas tree to start opening presents. The ripping and tearing of wrapping paper, mixed with laughter and *oohs* and *aahs* as everyone showed off their bounty, made for an exciting time.

I'm embarrassed to say that I lost my composure completely when I opened my gift from Wes's mother, Barbara. Carefully, I removed the red silk bow, opened up the box, and peeled back the clean white tissue paper.

Inside, I found an antique sterling silver baby cup and spoon that Wes's paternal grandmother had given to Barbara for Christmas twenty-nine years earlier, before she gave birth to Wes. A small card inside explained that it had been passed down for four generations, always at Christmas, and always to the eldest Radcliffe son and his wife.

I burst into tears.

"This is so special," I said. "I can't believe it. It's the best gift in the world, Barbara. I can't wait to put it to good use."

Wes, who sat next to me on the sofa, put his arm around me and kissed my forehead. "I love you, babe."

Everyone cheered and clapped, and more tears streamed down my cheeks.

"Not that we're pressuring you or anything," Barbara said over the hullabaloo as she passed me a box of Kleenex. "There's no rush. You two have plenty of time. You should enjoy these years of freedom before the babies arrive. I just want you to know that we're delighted to have you as a part of our family, Claire."

"I'm delighted, too," I replied, laughing with happiness through my tears. "I love you all. Merry Christmas!" I rose to my feet, stepped over the mountain of wrapping paper and glittery ribbons on the floor, and hugged Barbara in front of the tree.

Wes's father, George—a stern, serious man and natural patriarch of the family—forged a path through the mess and hugged me as well.

Later that afternoon, after a delicious lunch with the Radcliffes, Wes and I drove home to our cozy little craftsman style home in the South End. A fresh blanket of snow had fallen that morning, and the old sections of the city looked like something you'd see on the front of a Victorian Christmas card.

We pulled into our driveway and while Wes checked his phone for messages, I stepped out of the car to gaze up at the first stars visible in the sky. The moon was full and beginning its rise. It was a peaceful, quiet evening.

Closing my eyes, I breathed in the fresh winter air and made a wish.

I'm sure you know what I wished for...

I then turned and noticed that the house across the street—which had been listed for sale since before we purchased ours—was showing a SOLD sign.

"Look at that," I said. "It must be a Christmas miracle."

Wes stepped out of the car and turned to look. "Wow. It's about time. I thought that house would be on the market forever. I hope the new owners are up to the challenge."

From the outside, it was a charming, modest little craftsman like ours, but we had looked at it when we were house hunting, and it was dumpy on the inside—far more of a fixer-upper than we could handle.

"Maybe it was purchased by a contractor," I said, "and he's going to renovate it, flip it, and make a huge profit, because this is a pretty high-demand neighborhood. We probably should have thought of that ourselves."

Wes chuckled and shook his head. "If only I had the skills."

I laughed, because it was a running joke between us—how completely *un*handy Wes was around the house when it came to fixing things.

He pulled on his winter gloves and went to the shed in the backyard to fetch a shovel to clear the snow off the walk.

I carried our bags and gifts into the house, set

everything down and turned on the string of outdoor Christmas lights that decorated the covered veranda. Then I removed my coat and turned on the tree lights as well. Our cozy living room looked like a tiny piece of heaven—festive with the tree in the front window, a golden angel on top. Red and white felt stockings hung from the mantel beneath an array of lush evergreen boughs that scented the room with pine.

I lit a fire in the grate, then moved to the front window to see how Wes was doing with the shoveling.

"He's almost done," I said to myself.

With a happy sigh, I went to the kitchen to peel the aluminum foil off the small fruitcake one of his aunts had given us as we were walking out the front door of his parents' house. I bent forward to inhale the delectable aroma, then cut us each a slice. As soon as I heard Wes kicking the snow off his boots on the porch, I scooped some vanilla ice cream on top of each one.

The front door opened, and I had both plates ready for him as he entered the kitchen.

"That looks good." He gave me a kiss on the cheek.

"Your nose is cold," I replied with a grin.

He touched it with the tips of his fingers. "Is it? You're right. Just let me get my coat off. Is there any coffee?"

"I'll make some right now."

He turned away and a few minutes later, we sat down on the sofa, where we gobbled up the fruitcake while listening to Bing Crosby on the radio and watching the fire burn.

"It was a wonderful Christmas," I said, counting all my blessings.

He squeezed my hand.

We spent the evening lounging around in our pajamas and playing with the remote control helicopter that Bev had given to Wes for Christmas. He flew it into the Christmas tree, where it got stuck in the garland and sent us both into a fit of laughter.

When we finally untangled it, I took a turn and flew it into the ceiling fan, where it broke into a million pieces. We were lucky no one lost an eye.

"I don't know if we're ready to be parents," Wes said, laughing hysterically.

I laughed, too, as I grabbed the broom from the front closet and swept the wreckage off the floor. I was still laughing as I dumped it into the trash can. "We should have recorded that. It could have gone viral."

We laughed until we cried.

T wo months later, our new neighbors moved in across the street. We waited for the moving truck to leave, then gave them a few days to settle in before we walked over one afternoon with a plate of homemade cookies.

We climbed the steps and I reached up and rang the doorbell.

A woman answered. She was strikingly beautiful with long, dark, wavy hair and giant blue eyes. I guessed she was about thirty.

"Hi," I said. "We're your neighbors." I pointed at our house directly across the street. "That's our house right there. I'm Claire and this is Wes." I held out the cookies. "And this for you. Welcome to the neighborhood."

A man, who I presumed to be her husband, appeared in the doorway behind her. He, too, was extremely attractive in an artsy, intellectual way, with strong facial features, rimless eyeglasses, and tousled hair with hints of grey. It looked as if he had just stepped out of the shower because his hair was slightly damp. He wore a fisherman's knit sweater and khaki shorts with Birkenstocks, which I found rather odd, since it was not yet spring and there were still patches of snow on the ground.

The woman accepted my cookie offering. "Thank you so much. This is very sweet. Come in."

She stepped aside and opened the door to allow us to pass. We entered to discover that most of the unpacking was done—there were no boxes anywhere in sight. And the house had been completely renovated since our real estate agent had shown it to us the previous year. It now boasted a contemporary style decor with crisp white walls and dark hardwood floors, with plenty of light coming in from a wall of windows at the back. It looked like a brand new house, like something out of *Architectural Digest*.

Wes and I had watched the contractors coming and going over the past few months, but there had never been any sign of the new owners, so we'd assumed it was a real estate flip—until the snazzy Mercedes coupe pulled into the driveway, along with a brand new white Audi SUV. I wondered which one belonged to which partner.

"This is beautiful," I said, glancing up at the white-painted exposed beams on the vaulted ceilings.

"Thank you," the woman replied, "but we're still so disorganized." She held out her hand. "I'm Angie and this is Scott. It's nice to meet you both."

Scott shook our hands as well.

"So, how long have you been living in the neighborhood?" Scott asked as he led us to the white leather sofas in the living room, where a spectacular stone fireplace served as the focal point.

"Just over a year," I replied.

Wes went on to explain how much we both liked it, how it was wonderful that we could walk to the park, yet we were still close to downtown and all the restaurants on the waterfront.

Angie set the plate of cookies on the coffee table and peeled back the aluminum foil, then offered us tea or coffee or a glass of milk.

We all opted for coffee.

While she was in the kitchen—which was totally open concept—Scott asked what we both did. We told him we were teachers and that's how we'd met.

Scott then explained that he was an independent I.T. consultant and often traveled to different parts of the world to help companies upgrade their computer systems, while Angie was a clerk who'd just transferred to the payroll department in a Federal government office downtown.

I found it odd that he was a computer guy. I would have guessed a poet or an environmentalist. And I couldn't imagine Angie working in a cubicle in a government office. She looked like she belonged in a corner office on the top floor of a glass skyscraper. Or maybe on the cover of *Vogue*.

Together, they were a picture perfect couple.

"Where did you live before this?" I asked Scott.

"We had a condo in downtown Toronto," he replied, "but we wanted a slower paced lifestyle. You know what I mean... More birds and trees, less exhaust fumes. I was getting tired of the constant roar of traffic outside our window."

"*We?*" Angie said with a raised eyebrow as she placed our coffee cups on a silver tray and carried it to the living room.

I couldn't help but sense that she harbored some resentment about the move.

Scott gave us an apologetic smile. "Okay, Angie wasn't all that keen at first, but I think she's happy about it now. Right hon?"

"We'll see," she said, not giving him an inch. "Don't get me wrong. This is a beautiful city. I just wasn't happy about leaving my friends at work, because I'd been there almost ten years. At least I was able to get a transfer to Halifax, so I won't lose my pension or benefits."

As she set down the tray of coffee and took a seat beside me on the sofa, I could feel an intensity in her, along with a discord between her and her husband. Part of me wondered if we had interrupted them in the middle of an argument.

I glanced at Scott, whose body language seemed relaxed as he lounged back in the chair with one arm along the back of it.

"How long have the two of you been together?" I asked. "Do you have children?"

I hadn't seen any signs of a family, unless the kids were with their grandparents this week while Angie and Scott got settled. Secretly, I hoped they did have young children, so that ours would have playmates in the years to come.

"Not yet," Angie said. "Not that we haven't been trying." She gave Scott a chilly, almost contemptuous look.

An awkward silence ensued, so I leaned forward to pick up my coffee cup.

"We've been trying too, actually," I said, wanting to ease the tension. "No luck yet."

"How long?" Angie asked.

I shrugged a shoulder, as if I were barely keeping track. "Oh, I don't know. Just a few months."

I noticed Wes shift uncomfortably beside me and suspected he didn't want me to discuss something so personal with people we'd only just met, but it was too late now.

Angie waved a dismissive hand. "Oh, that's nothing. It's been two years for us."

Two years? This caused me some concern. "Really?"

"Yes, but Scott's away all the time. That kind of cuts your chances way down when you're not together when it matters…if you know what I mean."

Scott leaned forward and laid a hand on her knee. He rubbed it encouragingly. "That's part of the reason why I wanted to move out here—so that I could slow down and not travel so much." He smiled warmly at both of us. "The rat race can be a killer."

"I'm sure," Wes replied as he raised his coffee to his lips. "Well, now that you're here, I'm sure you'll love it. It's a good neighborhood and a terrific city. Great nightlife. Are you a runner, Scott? Because the park's really good for that."

Scott acknowledged the tip with a nod of his head, but I speculated that running probably wasn't his thing. "Thanks. Good to know."

We talked about some of our favorite restaurants and we told them where all the movie theatres were, and where the nearest gym was located. Scott wanted to know if we could recommend a good lawn and garden care company, but we couldn't because we'd always mowed our own lawn and pulled our own weeds.

After we finished our coffees, Wes and I stood up to let them get back to their unpacking, and we exchanged phone numbers.

As we crossed the street to return home, I asked Wes, "What did you think of them?"

He reached for my hand. "I don't know. Angie didn't seem too happy about being here. And Scott was clearly embarrassed when she brought up the fact that they'd been trying to have a baby for two years. Somebody needs to explain to her about filters."

I chuckled. "I'm sorry I got pulled into that."

"It wasn't your fault." Wes wrapped his arm around me. "Do you feel like ordering a pizza tonight?"

"Sounds perfect." We entered the house and he called the pizza shop.

—

My twenty-seventh birthday came and went, and still, I was not in the family way.

To try and relieve some of the stress I was feeling, I joined an evening yoga class with Angie from across the street. She told me it was a good way to keep our body rhythms moving in the right direction, in order to get pregnant. As a result, we started spending a lot of time together because we'd registered for three classes a week and we always went out for green tea afterward.

Eventually, because of what she'd told me the first time we met, I decided to confide in her about how disappointed I was that I hadn't gotten pregnant yet, and I asked her advice. I told her how badly I wanted to have a child. I even told her about losing my father when I was young, and how I had suffered from a fear of abandonment for many years until I met Wes. Now that we were having a bit of trouble getting pregnant, I worried that we would never have a family of our own, which I wanted more than anything. Not just for myself, but for Wes, because he had been an only child and it was his dream to have a house full of children.

Before I realized it, I was softly crying.

Angie laid her hand on top of mine. "Have you ever talked to your doctor about it?"

I shook my head. "No. I haven't wanted to admit to Wes

that there might be a problem—because I don't want to let him down. But I'm starting to feel really worried about it."

"It might not be your fault," she said. "*He* might be the one with the problem." She sat back and sipped her tea. "But seriously, how many months has it been? Six? It's not that bad. Some couples just take that long."

I nodded and blew my nose. "What about you and Scott? Have you seen a doctor about it?"

She exhaled heavily. "Yes, and we know exactly who's to blame."

"Really?"

She spoke matter-of-factly. "Scott's sperm count is okay, but they have poor motility."

I sat forward and whispered. "Does that mean he's sterile?"

A dozen other questions darted about in my brain, like what they planned to do if that was the case. Did they have a Plan B? Because I would be jumping on other options right away if I were in her shoes and knew what the problem was.

"No, he's not *completely* sterile," she replied, "but it just decreases our odds."

"Is there anything you can do to help things along?" I envisioned her standing on her head after sex. That's probably what I would do—anything to help those little swimmers reach the finish line.

"Yes," she replied, "and we're doing everything the doctor recommends. It just hasn't been enough. At least not yet, but it ain't over 'till it's over, right? Maybe this will be our year. And I'm not giving up, because Scott is my whole life. He's everything I've ever wanted, other than kids. I don't know how he puts up with me."

"I'll cross my fingers for you," I replied. "And you can cross yours for me at the same time."

Angie smiled and raised her teacup in salute, and I thought back to the first day we met.

I felt badly for judging her the way I did, thinking that she was intense and contemptuous. She was actually a very nice person. It was a good lesson for me—that sometimes first impressions about a person can be all wrong.

I was happy that she and Scott had become our new neighbors. There was just something about the timing of it...

I had several good friends, but their lives seemed on track, moving forward as they should. Having a friend in the same boat as me—another couple also having trouble getting pregnant—made me feel less alone. It was nice to have someone to talk to. Someone who understood.

"Just be careful," she said, "that you don't let this put stress on your marriage. It can really wreck your sex life if you get too uptight and impatient about it. That's something I've had to work on with Scott. He often has to remind me to relax. But he's incredibly patient with me. He understands why I get upset sometimes, and I love him for that."

I nodded and gazed out the window. "That's good advice," I said. "I'll keep it in mind."

But I couldn't imagine ever looking at my husband the way she had looked at Scott that first day, with a momentary flash of disdain. I simply loved Wes too much. He was my soul mate and my best friend, the most supportive husband in the world, and we were a team, no matter what. If it turned out that there *was* a problem—either with him or with me—I knew we would figure out how to deal with it.

Together.

Six

Two months later

"**M**aybe we should see someone," I carefully suggested to Wes as we sat together on the sofa one night, watching the evening news. "I've been doing everything right—eating well, taking my vitamins, and we've been trying at the right time of the month."

Wes leaned closer and laid his hand on my knee. "Don't worry, hon. Just be patient. It'll happen."

"But it's been almost eight months," I replied. "I'm trying not to get anxious, but it's hard sometimes. And if there is something wrong, wouldn't it be better for us to know now, so that we can start to do something about it?"

He nodded. "I totally agree, that we should take the bull by the horns if we need to, but realistically, I think we should give it a year before we start to panic."

"A *year*? Really?"

"Yes. Did you know that the opening to the cervix is about the same size as the tip of a straw? Seriously, what are the odds of hitting the jackpot every time? I don't know if my aim's that good. And you only ovulate once every thirty days. There are a lot of moving parts."

He was right, and I knew I needed to relax. I managed to chuckle, in an effort to lighten the mood, because I remembered Angie's advice about making sure I didn't create stress in my marriage. "Moving parts?"

Wes grinned and shrugged. "Maybe that's not the best choice of words. I'm just saying that it doesn't always happen right away. We just have to keep trying until we get lucky." He sipped his beer and returned his attention to the television screen. "Isn't there a way to take your temperature so we know exactly when you're ovulating?"

"I have been taking it," I confessed, "and I've made sure we do it at least once when I'm ripe, so to speak. Preferably twice."

He reached out to put his arm around me. I snuggled closer and rested my cheek on his shoulder.

"Don't worry," he said. "Everything will be fine."

I gazed up at his handsome profile and felt a wave of love move through me. "I don't know what I would do without you."

"I don't know either," he said with a grin.

We stopped talking about our baby-making efforts when breaking news appeared on the screen. There was torrential flooding in the southern U.S.

We were glued to the TV for hours.

Through the night, around 3:00 a.m., I woke up in a cold sweat after dreaming about a woman I had seen on one of the news segments. She had been trapped in her car as it floated down the street like a whitewater raft. A good Samaritan had rescued her with his speed boat, which he had stored in his driveway in a suburban neighborhood a few streets away.

In my dream, the woman had not been rescued. She had drowned because there was no good Samaritan nearby with a boat.

And in my dream, the woman was me.

CHAPTER

Seven

September arrived—marking the one-year anniversary since Wes and I had started trying to have a baby—and with it came my "monthly bill."

By this time, I had accepted the fact that fate was not simply going to hand me a golden ticket to motherhood right out of the gate, and despite my efforts to follow Angie's advice and not put stress on my marriage, our love life had taken a bit of a hit. Sex was no longer something we did to express our love for each other when we were in the mood. It had become an obligation. Sometimes even a chore.

Often, I would lay awake at night staring into the future, fearing that five more years would pass, and we would still be without children. I imagined myself continuing to take my temperature each month, forcing Wes into the bedroom at the right time, even when neither of us felt like it.

Surely if this continued, romance between us would no longer exist as we once knew it, and I didn't want that to happen.

To my credit, I made every effort *not* to behave in a clinical or hurried fashion when I knew I was ovulating. I lit candles and I wore sexy nighties, but it wasn't easy to be playful when fear was starting to take hold—fear that it might not *ever* happen for us.

I wish I could say that I was able to be patient, like Wes, and that I truly believed in my heart that it would happen when the time was right. But I *didn't* believe it. In fact, as the weeks passed, I felt more and more certain that something was terribly wrong, even though I had no proof.

Nevertheless, I couldn't help working myself up into a state of hopeful anticipation each month, which only made everything worse. I told myself: Surely the magic has happened at last and I'll finally be able to share the happy news that I'm in the family way.

My fantasies were elaborate.

"Do you want to know if it's a boy or a girl?" my mother would ask.

"No, we want it to be a surprise," I would reply.

Wes's parents would hug me, and George would pat Wes on the back and say, "Well done, Wes. Congratulations. You've made us both very happy."

There would be baby showers and books to read about baby care, Lamaze classes and prenatal vitamins, and morning sickness that I would *never* resent, not for a single moment. I *wanted* to feel sick. I daydreamed about how I would have to excuse myself from the classroom to rush to the washroom and find a toilet.

How crazy is that? Fantasizing about throwing up!

And I couldn't wait to gain weight and look at myself in the mirror and plan how I would lose it later. I would join one of those outdoor "new mommy" exercise classes with other young mothers, where we would meet in the park with our strollers, find a shady spot under some trees, and do squats and sit-ups while our babies watched from the cute flannel blankets we spread out on the grass.

I saw those mothers sometimes, when I was out for a run by myself on the weekends. I tried not to stare at them, but it wasn't easy. I wanted so badly to be among them.

Sometimes I closed my eyes and imagined myself cradling my sweet baby in my arms, rocking her back to sleep in the nursery after rising from bed in the middle of the night to change her diaper and feed her.

I shouldn't have let myself indulge in those fantasies. Angie told me not to because she said they would raise me to a very high place from which to fall each month.

Looking back on it, she was right about that. I wish I could have been less hopeful and less inclined to daydream. Maybe then, I might have been more aware of what was happening around me—and the fact that something was about to come down on my marriage like a sledgehammer.

Although, the blame can't be entirely laid at my feet. What happened was shocking and unbelievable. I don't think any normal person would have seen it coming.

"Well…" I said to Wes on our third anniversary, which we spent at home that year to save money. "It's been a whole year and we're still trying. Do you think it's time we go and see someone? Because I'd like to know if we're just spinning our wheels. Maybe we need some help."

It had been a number of weeks since I'd brought up the pregnancy issue with Wes. When my period started each month, I cried privately and quietly in the bathroom. Or I talked to Angie, who always understood, because she was going through the same thing. I did *not* make a point of announcing to Wes that we had failed. *Again and again.*

Wes didn't need me to tell him. He knew. He also understood that asking me about it would only rub salt in the wound. And of course he knew that I would tell him immediately if there was something good to report.

"Yes," he said at last. "I think it's time. Why don't you make the appointment." He reached across the breakfast table and squeezed my hand. "Don't worry, babe. I'm sure we just need to keep trying, but if you want me to get tested to make sure I'm not shooting blanks, I'm totally willing to do that."

"It might not be you," I said. "It could be me."

He lowered his gaze to his plate of scrambled eggs and poked at it with his fork. "Whatever it is, we'll deal with it." He said nothing for a moment or two, then his eyes lifted. "And let's not obsess about whether it's you or me. We're a team and we're in this together."

I felt a surge of relief—that he was willing to explore what might be wrong. I loved that we were about to become pro-active, because the last thing I wanted was to continue to feel so powerless—as if the possibility of having a child was completely out of our hands. Surely there were things we could do to increase our chances of making it happen. Surely it wasn't all up to fate?

On top of that, if there *was* something wrong with one of us, medically, we needed to get help and not waste time, because I wasn't getting any younger. I hated to say it—it sounded so cliché—but I could feel the clock starting to tick, and it made me nervous. Maybe even a little frantic.

Thank God I had Angie to talk to. She was the only person who really understood.

Eight

Wes and I started out by booking an appointment with my family doctor, who assured us that we had done the right thing to wait a year before coming to see her. She explained that it's not uncommon for couples not to conceive right away. But often, they grow antsy after only a few months, in which case she advised them to keep trying and come back after a year if they still weren't pregnant.

I laughed. "Actually, I wanted to come after three months, but Wes convinced me to keep trying a little while longer."

Dr. Melanson smiled at him. "Don't fault her for being a keener."

He reached for my hand. "I never would."

Dr. Melanson regarded us both for a few seconds. I had the distinct impression she was gauging the strength of our relationship, and whether or not we were having sex in the first place. Which we were.

She wheeled her chair forward a bit and picked up her pen to take some notes in our file. "Let's get right down to it then." She turned her eyes to me. "First of all, Claire. Do you have regular periods?"

"Yes," I replied. "It's like clockwork every month, and I've been taking my temperature to figure out when I'm ovulating. I read that it happens between day ten and seventeen of the cycle."

She nodded and wrote that down. "Very good. Clearly you've been educating yourself." She glanced back and forth between the two of us. "And how often do you have sex?"

I blushed, and Wes grinned sheepishly at me.

"I'm not here to judge you," Dr. Melanson said. "And all of this is strictly confidential. I just need to know the facts."

I took a deep breath and sat up straighter. "Usually about three times a week. Sometimes only twice if we're busy at the school. But when I'm ovulating, we make sure to do it every other day."

"Excellent," she said, noting that in the file.

Dr. Melanson then asked us a few more detailed questions about our sex life, which I won't repeat here. Eventually she moved on to explain what we should expect from these appointments, and what would happen next.

"First, we'll deal with you, Wes, and get a sperm sample. Incidentally, just so you know, we're not here to point fingers at either of you. Statistically speaking, one third of couples have an infertility problem involving the male, while one third of the problems involve the female, and another third involve both. So that's why we need to examine each of you, individually."

"Interesting," I said, pleased to hear that Wes and I were on equal footing, at least statistically.

Dr. Melanson seemed a bit distracted as she wrote something down on a separate sheet of pink paper, which she handed to Wes. "This is a requisition for you to provide a sperm sample. You can do that in the next few days. The instructions are on the sheet and there's a number to call. And Wes…I'd like to see you back here in two weeks for a complete physical."

"Sure," he said, taking the sheet of paper from her.

"What about me?" I asked. "Aren't there any tests I should be taking? Or are there some fertility drugs we should be looking at?"

Dr. Melanson rose from her chair and handed me a sheet of paper as well. "Let's take this one step at a time. For now, I want to get your blood work done, Claire, and I'd like to book you in for a physical as well. But I would like to have the results of Wes's sperm test before I see either of you again. Why don't you book separate appointments on the same day two weeks from now? I'll have more information then, and we can figure out how to move forward. In the meantime, just try to relax and keep doing what you've been doing."

Wes and I stood up.

"Thank you," I said as we walked out.

When we reached our car, I threw my arms around Wes's neck, because I felt elated. Even though we had no information yet, I was grateful that someone was going to look into our situation, medically, and figure out what was wrong, if anything.

At the same time, I was still impatient. I wished I didn't have to wait two whole weeks before we could return for our physicals and get the results from Wes's sperm test. I wanted things to move much faster than that.

After two weeks twiddling my thumbs, waiting in suspense

to return to the clinic for back-to-back appointments, the day finally arrived.

Wes was called in first, so I was forced to sit and wait a little longer. It was torture.

Finally, he emerged from the examination room and sat down beside me.

I closed the thriller novel I'd been trying to read and held it on my lap. "Well?"

"It went great," he told me.

"Really? What did she say?"

He leaned closer and spoke softly. "That my sperm count is off the charts, and motility is terrific. Everything looks really good."

I let out a breath and sat back. "Phew. That's a relief. So at least we're all good on your end. One less thing to worry about."

"I'm sure you'll be fine, too." Wes pulled out his phone to check his messages. "And if there's anything wrong, they'll be able to help us. Like you said, you might just need to take some fertility drugs to increase our chances. Or maybe this is the week we'll get lucky and they'll be referring us to an obstetrician on the next visit."

He said that because I was ovulating this week. We had done it twice the night before, and I was hopeful, as always.

A nurse entered the waiting room and called my name. I rose from my seat and shoved my book into my purse.

"Wish me luck," I said to Wes as I followed the nurse into the examination room.

It was an interesting visit with Dr. Melanson.

First she took my blood pressure. It was a very healthy 118 over 79. She then went over my blood work, and the results were perfect. I wasn't surprised, as I'd never had any health issues before. I ate well and got plenty of exercise. Other than having some trouble getting pregnant, I felt great.

She then asked me a number of questions while taking notes in my file. We discussed my family's medical history and allergies and all the other things doctors usually ask. Then my answer to one particular question caused her to look up from the chart and study me more intently.

"You were thrown from a horse?" she asked. "When did this happen?"

I cleared my throat and strove to provide the sorts of details she might be looking for.

"I was fourteen years old. It was one of those public trail rides at a farm somewhere in the boonies, but the horse I was on got spooked for some reason and just started bucking all over the place. I was knocked unconscious and I had to have surgery so they could fix my bladder."

She lowered her gaze and wrote that down.

"That farm doesn't offer trail rides anymore," I added.

She started writing faster, and it seemed she was already forming some conclusions. I started to feel a little sick. My heart pounded hard in my chest.

Could this be the reason why I wasn't getting pregnant? Was I a lost cause?

She set the chart down on her desk and met my gaze.

"The first thing I want to do," she said, "is refer you to an excellent gynecologist. She's a fertility specialist, and she'll arrange for you to have an ultrasound to see how things look."

"What will that show?" I asked, struggling not to reveal my concern that something was wrong with me and it was not fixable.

"We'll be looking for unusual growths or tumors," she explained. "Don't worry. It's a standard test we do, just to rule things out. After that, you can meet with Dr. Walker for the results and she'll take over from there."

"Okay," I replied, feeling uncomfortable that she was passing me on to someone else, further up the chain. Clearly mine was looking to be a complicated case.

"I can try to get you in next week," she said, looking back down at the chart.

"Okay, but am I all right?" I asked. "Do you think something's wrong with me? Is it because I fell off that horse?"

Dr. Melanson gave me a compassionate smile and laid a hand on my knee. "Please try not to worry, Claire. We don't know anything for sure yet, but we'll figure it out, one step at a time. You'll be in good hands with Dr. Walker. She's amazing. She's going to do everything she can to help you."

Help me?

Certainly, that's why I was there. I wanted help. But when Dr. Melanson put it like that…I felt like I was back in that nightmare, drowning in a flood, and I was beginning to panic.

Another week of excruciating suspense passed by at a snail's pace. It was pure torture because I couldn't help but assume the worst—that I was totally barren because of the trauma I had suffered as a teen.

After talking to Angie about it after our next yoga class, I began to research the subject on the Internet. Some of what I read boosted my spirits, while other bits of information only made me feel more worried and pessimistic.

I was desperate for answers and frustrated by the fact that I was completely powerless to make things move any faster. I even tried calling the doctor's office to see if they could fit me in sooner for the ultrasound, but they couldn't do it. They were booked solid.

"You need to relax about all this," Wes said to me one night when he came home from the gym and found me sitting in the dark, at the desk in the spare bedroom with the laptop open in front of me.

"I can't," I replied, not turning around or rising to greet him, because I had just clicked on an interesting link I wanted to follow. "I'm just so worried that something's wrong with me. I can't explain it, but I have a bad feeling."

He approached and stood behind me. "This is the age of modern medicine. I'm sure they'll be able to fix whatever's wrong."

"Maybe." I started reading the information on the website home page as soon as it opened in front of me.

Wes exhaled heavily and turned away. A moment later, I heard him in the kitchen, making something to eat. He was slamming cupboard doors.

Realizing I'd been distracted when he came in, I closed my laptop, rose from my chair, and went into the kitchen.

"How was your workout?" I carefully asked.

"Fine," he tersely replied.

I frowned as I watched him move around the kitchen, because this wasn't like him, to be so visibly irritable.

"You seem angry," I said.

He glanced at me briefly and merely shrugged as he slapped peanut butter on a slice of bread, practically ripping it to shreds with the knife.

I was surprised and baffled because he never behaved this way. I wasn't even sure what was wrong—only that his aggravation seemed to come out of left field. Sure…I may have been a bit preoccupied lately, but certainly it wasn't enough to warrant this sudden cold shoulder treatment.

All I wanted to do was resolve whatever the problem was, so I spoke calmly. "I'm sorry if I've been distracted lately. It's just that…" I moved a little closer. "I'm starting to get a bit scared that it's never going to happen for us, that I'm never going to be able to give you children, and I know how much it means to you. To both of us. Is that why you're upset? Because we've hit some roadblocks?"

Wes wouldn't look at me as he moved to the fridge. He pulled out a carton of milk and poured himself a glass.

"I'm just getting tired of this, Claire. You've been completely obsessed." He shook his head. "We don't talk about anything except fertility and your ovulatory cycle, and all the worst case scenarios—like years going by and the two of us still being childless. 'Oh, woe is me.' Seriously, Claire? If you ask me, the reason we can't get pregnant has nothing to do with infertility. It's because you're so stressed out about it. There's probably nothing wrong with you. I wish you'd just relax and let nature take its course." He rolled his eyes. "And don't even get me started on our sex life."

I stood in shock as he strode past me to the living room. Never once in our marriage had he spoken to me like that, nor had he ever expressed any frustration or discontent about our situation. He'd always been supportive and optimistic.

He flopped down on the sofa, put his feet up on the coffee table, and picked up the remote control. He turned on a football game.

I followed him and tried to make sense of everything he had just said to me.

"I didn't know you felt this way," I said.

"Well, I do."

I was quiet for a moment while my heart began to pound. I felt completely blindsided by this sudden change in him. "I know our sex life hasn't exactly been normal lately. Do you want to talk about it?"

He inclined his head at me, glaring. "No. I don't want to talk to you, Claire. I just want to watch the game."

His animosity was like a punch in the stomach. All of a

sudden, he was a stranger to me, not the loving husband I knew. I was speechless.

He bit into his bread and watched the TV screen, ignoring me.

"I'm sorry," I said, sitting down on the sofa beside him, because I couldn't just walk away and leave things like this. We'd never talked to each other this way. *Ever.*

"I honestly didn't know you were unhappy," I said. "I promise I'll try to lighten up, and I'm sure I'll feel better after the ultrasound, when I finally know what's going on. And maybe you're right. Maybe there's nothing wrong with me, and we just haven't gotten lucky yet."

Even as I spoke the words, I didn't believe them, because my intuition had been poking at me for a while now. I couldn't shake the feeling that something was wrong with me. I was only saying these things to smooth things over between Wes and me, because I didn't want to go to bed angry.

"Let's just forget about it, okay?" he said. "I'm sick of discussing it. And I don't want to talk about our sex life either. It is what it is."

Still in shock from this abrupt change in him, I rose from the sofa. "All right then. I'll leave you alone."

I walked out and he didn't follow, nor did he come to bed that night. He fell asleep on the sofa with the television on, and that's where he stayed.

The following morning, while we were getting ready for work, he apologized for the things he'd said, but his mood remained irritable and standoffish. I didn't understand how he could become such a different person overnight. It was like suddenly being married to Dr. Jekyll and Mr. Hyde.

At the same time, I worried that it was my fault—that I

had been too preoccupied lately and had missed all the signals. That my husband wasn't happy and I'd been too self-absorbed to notice.

We didn't speak to each other at work that day. Not once. Not even during lunch hour, which used to be the time when we met up for a chat, and flirt or sneak a kiss in the teachers' lounge if no one was around.

That night, when Wes slid into bed, he shut off the light right away and said, "Let's just take a break from trying this week, okay? Since you're not ovulating anyway."

"Okay," I replied, feeling hurt and rejected as he turned his back on me and pulled the covers up to his neck.

Suddenly, a crushing fear came down upon me as I remembered how I had felt on the day I watched the paramedics wheel my father into the back of the ambulance. My life had fallen apart in a matter of hours and there had been no warning.

Was that what was happening now? Was the good in my life about to be torn away?

I told myself I was being paranoid and overly sensitive, and I just needed to give Wes some space. I wasn't the only one who was worried about never having a family. He wanted children, too—as badly as I did—and I suspected he was tired of always having to be my rock.

I resolved to make more of an effort not to be pessimistic about our fertility issues, and I hoped that when I had more information from Dr. Walker—and hopefully a game plan—the pressure would ease off both of us.

The next day, I suggested to Wes that we go to a movie, which we did that night, and I also raised the idea of going away for March break in the spring. I thought it might be fun to start planning a trip somewhere exotic and romantic.

Somewhere we'd never been before. Maybe a Caribbean cruise or a trip to Mexico? We could invite Angie and Scott to join us.

Wes seemed to like the idea, so it provided us with something to talk about, other than our problems conceiving a child.

On a more positive note, the ultrasound the following week did not reveal any unusual growths or tumors in my feminine parts, so that was good news.

And Dr. Walker turned out to be a lovely female OBGYN who made me feel at ease as soon as I entered her office.

She was young and pretty with long red curly hair—not much older than me—and she was the kind of person who was born to be a physician, for not only was she incredibly knowledgeable, she was also kind and caring. In the first five minutes, I felt as if I could tell her anything and confess my deepest fears. I sensed that she would be understanding and sympathetic, and offer helpful solutions.

She was completely transparent and told me what to expect at every turn from that moment on. Not only did she tell me *what* we were going to do, she told me *why* we were going to do it.

"So now that we've determined that there are no growths visible from the ultrasound," she said, "we need to look for any lingering effects from that fall you had when you were fourteen. Unfortunately, that kind of scarring wouldn't show up in the ultrasound."

"How will we look for that?" I asked.

She leaned back in her chair in a relaxed fashion, as if we were two close friends having coffee together, and said, "I'd like to book you in for a hysteroscopy and laparoscopy. These are scopes we can do to determine if your fallopian tubes are open wide enough for your eggs to pass through each month, from your ovaries down to your uterus. In your case, there's a chance that the trauma and surgery that occurred when you fell from the horse might have resulted in some scar tissue that's created an obstacle course for your eggs."

I blinked a few times. "Will I be awake for the scope?"

"No, we'll put you under, and it's a very simple procedure. We'll make a tiny incision right here." She showed me the spot near her own belly button. "And then we'll go in with the scopes and inject some dye into the tubes to see if they're clear."

"What if I *do* have scar tissue?" I asked. "What if my tubes are completely blocked? Is there any cure for that?"

She smiled warmly at me. "There are all sorts of options for every scenario, Claire, and we'll work through it together, I promise. In terms of what I think we might be dealing with here—if that old trauma is truly what's causing your difficulties in conceiving—how we treat it will depend on how much scarring there is. If there are only minor adhesions, we can clear it up during this procedure. Fertility drugs may or may not be needed."

"What if it's *not* minor?" I asked.

She spoke matter-of-factly, as if she weren't concerned in the least. "Then, there are still other options."

"Like what?"

She sat forward. "Well…we can consider IVF."

"In vitro fertilization?" I was actually thrilled to hear her speak of it, because I had been reading up on it and I had a good feeling about it.

Dr. Walker nodded. "I take it you're familiar."

"Yes, I've been doing research. It's when you harvest the woman's egg and inject the father's sperm to fertilize it. Then you put the embryo back into the woman's uterus so that the egg can implant there."

"That's right," she replied, looking impressed. "But with IVF—just like in a natural conception—not every embryo implants successful and results in a pregnancy. For a woman your age, it's about a fifty-fifty success rate. That's why we try to enhance those odds by freezing surplus embryos so that we can try again later if the first one doesn't take." She smiled at me. "But let's not get ahead of ourselves. We don't even know if that will be necessary. We need to get a look at your fallopian tubes first. Then we'll be able to formulate a plan. I'm going to try to get you in before Christmas."

We chatted for a few more minutes, then I stood up, feeling rejuvenated and far more positive than I had in months. I felt as if Dr. Walker was an angel sent from heaven, delivering a big, fat basket of hope to my doorstep.

I couldn't wait to go home and tell Wes. It had been a while since we'd done anything celebratory together. I decided to pick up a bottle of wine on the way home and cook his favorite meal.

My relationship with Wes took a turn for the better when I came home from my appointment with Dr. Walker and told him everything she had said. We talked over the dinner table where he apologized again for the way he had behaved that other night, and he promised it wouldn't happen again.

"You didn't deserve that," he said. "You're the most amazing woman in the world. I was a total jerk and I know it. I guess I just hit a wall."

I told him I understood, because it was a stressful situation.

I then assured myself that it was an ordinary, run-of-the-mill rough patch, and no marriage was perfect 365 days a year. There were bound to be ups and downs and I couldn't let every speed bump send me into that dark place where I feared everything I loved was going to be suddenly ripped out from under me.

And though it was usually Angie I talked to about our struggles to conceive a child, I had also been confiding in my sister, Bev. I had told her about my argument with Wes, which had left me heartbroken and confused that night.

Although Bev didn't have the same insights Angie did about these types of marital stresses, Bev was supportive. She was my sister and she loved me. We had been through a lot together and I knew she always had my back.

Maybe that's why it came as a surprise when she didn't show up at the hospital on the day I was scheduled to have my scope. It was a week before Christmas, and she had told me earlier that she would be there.

When the day finally arrived, all I received from her was a text, where she apologized for not being able to come, but she didn't say why. She merely said "good luck," which I found strange and worrisome. I tried to call her but she didn't answer her phone.

Wes, on the other hand, was there at my side, dutiful and supportive as always.

My mother came by as well, which I appreciated when I woke up and was wheeled out of recovery. It was good to have my husband and mother in the room with me when Dr. Walker entered with the results.

Dressed in blue scrubs and running shoes, her curly hair pulled back in a ponytail and a stethoscope slung around her neck, Dr. Walker said hello to Wes and my mom. Then she asked if I wanted to be told the results in private.

The question sent dread into my core.

"It's fine," I told her. "My mom and my husband will need to hear it eventually. So they might as well hear it from you."

"Okay." She took a seat in the chair next to my bed just as a man in a Santa Claus suit walked by outside the door.

"*Ho Ho Ho!*"

It was an odd moment under the circumstances, but this was the obstetrics floor and there were new mothers with babies in many of the rooms. I tried to take Santa as a good sign.

Dr. Walker smiled and rolled her eyes playfully. "We'll be seeing that guy every day for the next week. He comes every year and he's very jolly."

"That's nice," I said.

She nodded and continued. "So, I suspect that what I'm about to tell you about the procedure won't come as a total surprise, Claire. I've gotten a sense that you've had some suspicions for a while."

I swallowed uneasily and said, "Yes."

"Well." She kept her eyes fixed on mine as she let out a breath. "You were right. Now that I've had a chance to see how things look, it's no wonder you've been having trouble conceiving. Your tubes are completely blocked."

I shut my eyes and tried not to panic. It was not the news I had wanted to hear, yet it gave me some peace of mind to know that there was, in fact, a real problem, and that I hadn't been imagining it, as Wes had suggested. And Dr. Walker was here to help.

I tried to sit up straighter against the pillows, while my mother and Wes stood against the far wall.

"You mentioned a while ago," I said to Dr. Walker, "that if there was scarring, it might be possible to clear the way during the procedure."

She sat forward in the chair with her elbows on her knees, her hands clasped together. "Yes, I did say that, but in your case, I'm afraid it wasn't possible. The scarring is too severe. We wouldn't have been able to fix things."

My throat closed up, but I swallowed hard because I didn't want to cry. There would be other options. She had told me that in her office weeks ago.

"So…what has been happening to my eggs each month if they can't travel down my fallopian tubes? Where do they go?"

Dr. Walker gave me the facts. "They simply get absorbed into your body."

"I see." Clearing my throat, I formed my next wary question. "So where do we go from here?"

My mother and Wes said nothing, and part of me wished my husband were more involved in this conversation. I wished he had been the one to ask that question.

Dr. Walker laid her hand on my wrist. "You and your husband should definitely take some time to think about all this, but in my professional opinion, your best option is IVF. There are no guarantees, of course, and it's important that you keep that in mind, but I see no reason why we can't try for that. You're completely healthy in every other way. You're a good candidate, Claire."

Her words filled me with elation, because at least now, I had a fighting chance and science was on my side. There was a fifty-fifty success rate for women my age. She had told me that in her office and I had confirmed it in my online research.

Thank Heavens! Now we knew what the obstacle was, and there was a clear detour we could take around it.

How I loved the miracle of modern medicine in that moment—and the fact that I had an amazing specialist on my side. A brilliant woman who had the tools and expertise to help us.

I grabbed hold of her hand and squeezed it. "Thank you

so much, Dr. Walker. I can't tell you how happy you've made me. This is the best Christmas present ever. And if I have a girl, I want to name her after you."

Dr. Walker laughed. "That is so sweet, Claire. But really, that's not necessary. You should name your child whatever you want. I won't hold you to that promise."

I realized, when my mother began digging through her purse for something, that she was laughing and crying at the same time, searching for a tissue. This was such wonderful news!

Wes, on the other hand, had been checking his phone. When at last he met my gaze, he shook his head as if to clear it, then he moved around the bed and took hold of my hand.

"At least now we know," he said, glancing briefly at Dr. Walker and giving her a nod, which I took to mean a quiet thank you, even though I was dismayed by how uninvolved he had been during the entire conversation. It left me feeling cold inside.

"*Ho Ho Ho! Merry Christmas!*"

We all glanced up as Santa Claus walked by the door again, ringing his bell.

Wes smiled at me then, and patted my hand. "'Tis the season to be jolly," he said with a lightness in his tone that did not ease my concerns.

Not long after Dr. Walker left my room, I pulled out my cell phone and texted Bev.

Hey, it went well. Dr. Walker figured out the problem and we're going to deal with it. Things are looking up.

She texted me back: *That's great. I'm so relieved. When do you get to go home?*

I quickly thumbed a reply: *They'll be discharging me this afternoon. Do you want to come over for supper so I can fill you in? Wes is coaching a basketball game until nine.*

Bev didn't respond right away, and I found myself picking up my phone and checking it every few seconds, wondering what was going on, because something felt off.

Then I started to wonder if I was becoming paranoid about *everyone* in my life, constantly waiting for the other shoe to drop.

I knew where those feelings were coming from, and I didn't want to go through my entire life expecting everyone I loved to fall on hedge clippers.

At last, a message came in: *Sure. What time? I'll bring food so you don't have to cook.*

I typed my reply: *Great. How about 7:00?*
Sounds good. See you then.

CHAPTER

Twelve

My sister and her dog Leo arrived on my doorstep that night with a warm, roasted chicken and pre-made salad from the grocery store, along with homemade frosted sugar cookies in a Christmas candy tin.

I invited them inside, and we sat down on the sofa to eat in the living room in front of the tree, with our plates on our laps and Leo at our feet.

"Tell me exactly what Dr. Walker told you," Bev said as she sipped her water. "I'm dying to know."

I explained my prognosis to her—that what I had suspected all along wasn't just in my mind. I truly was incapable of conceiving naturally.

"What did Wes say about it?" Bev asked. "Did he feel badly for doubting you?"

I inhaled deeply. "He already apologized for that, but he was strangely calm about the whole thing. It's funny... I was weirdly overjoyed when Dr. Walker explained everything to me. It was just so nice to have a concrete answer and know what we were dealing with. And to learn how we could move forward. But Wes didn't seem happy at all. He just seemed kind of...*indifferent*. Like he didn't care. He barely seemed to be paying attention."

I shook my head and poked at my salad. "I don't know, Bev. I'm trying not to be paranoid, but I feel like there's a sudden disconnect in my marriage." I glanced up. "This past year definitely took a toll on us. Everything used to be so romantic and we were a team from day one, but somewhere along the line, he seems to have lost interest in having a baby, and it happened really fast. And he hasn't told his family anything about our troubles conceiving. His mother doesn't know, although she must suspect something."

"He does love you," Bev said. "I'm sure of it. He's always been supportive, right?"

"He was," I replied, "but that night when he came home and expressed his frustrations, it was like someone flipped a switch. He became this other person I didn't recognize. It made me wonder if he's been faking his love for me all along, and now that the going has gotten a bit tough with fertility issues, he suddenly wants out."

Bev reached for the bottle of salad dressing on the coffee table. "I think it's pretty typical," she said, as she squeezed the last of the dressing onto her plate, "for infertility to put strain on a marriage. Especially in the bedroom. I'm sure you guys aren't the first couple to feel this way. But at least now you know exactly what's wrong, and you can start to enjoy your sex life again, with no pressure. Dr. Walker can help you start your family in her clinic, and life will begin to feel more normal at home. You'll probably bond in a whole new way during that experience."

"I hope so." I finished my dinner and set the empty

plate on the coffee table. "Normal sounds great. I just want to go back to the way things were, when we were excited about starting a family together, and we were affectionate with each other. Remember last Christmas? I was so happy and he seemed happy, too. But then again, I thought I might be pregnant. It wasn't quite so magical on New Year's Eve when I realized I wasn't."

Bev sighed and touched my hand. "But now you have a plan. Maybe, by this time next year, you'll be as big as a barn, waddling around in stretchy maternity pants, eating for two."

I chuckled. "One can hope."

Bev was quiet for a moment. Then she set her empty plate on the coffee table and patted Leo, who had strolled over to sniff her plate. She set it on the floor to let him lick it. "Listen, I'm sorry for not being there for you today. I know it was a big deal and I promised I would come."

She seemed like she wanted to confess something.

"What happened?" I asked.

Bev stood up, collected our plates, and carried them to the kitchen while Leo trotted after her.

Though it caused me some discomfort physically, as I was still sore from the procedure, I rose from the sofa to follow, and found her rinsing our plates at the sink and loading them in the dishwasher. By then, Leo was lying down by the back door.

"I didn't know how to tell you," she said when she noticed me standing there. "That's why I've been a bit...out of touch the past few weeks."

"How to tell me *what*?" I asked.

Recognizing that I was slightly hunched over, Bev gave me a sympathetic look. "Oh gosh, Claire. You didn't need to get up. I was going to come straight back. I thought I'd make us some tea."

"Well…you can't walk out of a room with a cliff-hanger like that and expect me not to follow."

Bev closed the dishwasher door and rested her jean-clad hip against the counter. She stared at me for a moment, then without warning, burst into tears.

I rushed forward and laid a hand on her shoulder. "Oh, God. What's wrong? It can't be that bad."

She straightened and labored to collect herself. "I just didn't know how to tell you," she sobbed.

My stomach exploded with dread as a number of horrific possibilities dashed through my mind. Did Bev have a terminal disease? Was Mom dying? Or had Bev seen Wes somewhere with another woman, cheating on me?

"Why?" I asked. "You know you can tell me anything."

Bev let out a miserable laugh as she wiped her eyes with the backs of her hands. "It just seems so unfair. For the past year you've been telling me how badly you want to have a baby, but you kept hitting roadblock after roadblock, and you were so disappointed every month when it didn't happen." She paused.

"Go on," I said.

She struggled to take a breath, moved to the table and sat down. "I don't exactly know where to begin. Okay. A while ago, I met this guy at a party and we really hit it off. He was good looking and…well, you know I never do that sort of thing, but he looked so great in his faded blue jeans. I went back to his hotel afterwards—

"*His hotel?*"

Bev tried to make light of it. "He was from Ontario, here for a conference, and… Oh, it's hard to say this out loud, but…we spent the weekend together and…" She let out a breath. "*Oh, God.* I'm pregnant."

I blinked a few times, not sure I'd heard her correctly. "You're *pregnant?* Who is this guy? And I thought you were on the pill."

"I was," she replied, "but I haven't been for a while. Not since Jeff and I broke up. I knew I wasn't going to be intimate with anyone else until I was back in a committed relationship, but I've been single for a long time, and then… *Oh*…I don't know what happened, Claire. He was great, but it was totally irresponsible of me."

"Did you use any protection at all?" I asked, shocked that this could have happened to my baby sister who had always been such a goody-two-shoes. Her longtime boyfriend Jeff had been her high school sweetheart, and they'd been together for six years. Until recently, he was the great love of her life and the only man she had ever been with. *Ever.*

Until Mr. Handsome-Party-Pants came along.

"Of course we used protection," she replied. "But evidently, it's only 97% effective."

I shook my head in disbelief. "Humor me, please. I just want to make sure I understand what happened. He didn't pressure you, did he? Or force himself on you? Because if that's what happened—"

"Goodness no," she replied, waving a hand through the air and leaning forward on her elbows. "It was totally consensual. Actually, *I* was the one who suggested we go back to his hotel. I don't know what came over me. You're probably shocked."

I swallowed uneasily and sat down on a kitchen chair across from her.

Wow. My sister hadn't even *wanted* to get pregnant. She'd used protection but it had happened anyway. Meanwhile, I'd been taking my temperature and dragging my husband to the bedroom at exactly the right time each month and…*nothing.*

It *was* pretty unfair. But it wasn't Bev's fault.

I lifted my gaze. "How far along are you?"

"Two months."

Two months?

I stared at her in disbelief. "I can't believe you didn't tell me."

"Me neither," she replied, "but we haven't seen as much of each other lately, since you've been going to yoga classes with Angie. You don't call as often as you used to, so there just wasn't an opportunity. Besides, I was embarrassed that I had gone home with a guy I barely knew. I was mortified, to be honest. Then, when I realized I was pregnant, I couldn't come to you, because I knew how hard you'd been trying. I wasn't even sure if I was going to have it."

I shot her a look. "*What?*"

She gestured toward me. "See? That's why I couldn't tell you. I knew you'd freak out if you knew I was actually considering *not* having it."

I buried my face in my hands, then looked up again. "Of course I would have freaked out! Because you *have* to keep it, Bev. When you think about how desperately I've wanted to get pregnant, and how hard it's going to be for us…you can't just throw a blessing like that out the window."

She rested her forehead on the heel of her hand, and I could see how stressed she was, and it was obvious that she she'd been struggling with this issue for a while.

"Everyone isn't you, Claire. Every woman isn't going

through what you're going through. Some of us have very different issues to deal with." She dropped her gaze to her lap. "God, this is so messed up."

We sat in silence, neither of us saying a word.

Finally, Bev dried her eyes and stood up to put the kettle on to boil. Leo continued to sleep on the floor by the back door.

"All that aside," she said. "At the end of the day, what matters is that I finally figured out what was best for me. I knew I had to have it, no matter what the future held. I even considered the possibility of asking you to adopt her—or him. I thought maybe it was some kind of divine intervention… That I'd be able to give you what you want. But as the days and weeks passed, I realized I couldn't possibly give up my baby. Not for anyone. I want to have her and keep her and raise her. Even if I have to do it alone, I'll find a way."

It was unbelievable, what my sister had just revealed to me. And even though it was unfair, I understood that this was the way the world worked. Sometimes life is unfair, but all we can do is figure out a way to get through the hardships and keep on living—and loving the people who are important to us.

I stood up to join Bev at the counter, where she was dropping teabags into a couple of mugs. "You won't have to do this alone," I said. "I'll be there for you. You know that, right?"

She nodded and hugged me.

When we stepped apart, I said, "I can't imagine what you must have been going through. Have you told Mom?"

"Not yet."

I let out a breath. "Don't worry, she'll be fine about it.

You're twenty-five years old. It's not like you're in high school—and I promise, I'll have your back."

Bev hugged me again. "Thanks sis." Then she turned to pour the boiling water into the mugs.

"What about the father?" I asked. "Does he know?"

"No," she replied, "and I don't intend to tell him. It was just a wild weekend, and then he went back to Ontario."

"You haven't spoken to him since?"

"We texted a few times," she said, "but I didn't want to push for any kind of commitment after he left. And I really don't know him that well, so I'm not comfortable about bringing a stranger into my life who might turn out to be a terrible father figure for my child." She regarded me sheepishly. "That's probably selfish."

"No, it's not," I replied. "It's responsible, and I understand. But he probably has some legal rights. You might want to talk to a lawyer."

Bev shook her head with regret as she picked up her mug, took the teabag by the string and bobbed it up and down. "I never imagined anything like this would ever happen to me, but I have to admit, I'm not sorry." She met my eyes. "I've had time to think about it, and I want to have this baby. Even if it's challenging and difficult as a single mom..." She laid her hand on her belly. "This little person is a part of me now, and I'm already in love. I never knew I could feel like this."

I exhaled a long sigh of contentment. "You don't have to explain. I understand. And maybe some day we're going to look back on this moment and say, 'That was the best Christmas ever—the year all the miracles happened.'"

"You think so?"

"I do, because I have a good feeling about where things

are going from here. Last year, I had no idea how hard it was going to be, but now, here we are. You're going to have a baby, and I have an amazing doctor who's going to circumvent my blocked fallopian tubes and help Wes and me start a family. As far as I'm concerned, this is already the best Christmas ever."

We moved back into the living room, where the white tree lights were reflecting like starlight in the front window. I smiled at Bev as we sat down.

"I can't wait to be Auntie Claire to your beautiful baby. And you'll get to be Auntie Bev when my turn comes around. I can just see us now, taking our babies for walks together in our strollers, and commiserating when they start school and leave the nest. They'll grow up together as cousins, and we'll always be together."

Bev began to cry again, but this time, with happy tears as Leo trotted in and rested his chin on her lap. "You're the best sister ever. I don't know what I would do without you."

I felt blissful and alive, because with Bev's news, I'd already received a precious gift, even though Christmas Day was still a week off.

It was true that life didn't always go according to plan, but I was ready to do whatever it took to conceive a child and restore my marriage to what it was. There were only good times ahead. I had modern medicine on my side to overcome the obstacles that stood in the way of Wes and me having a family together. And I had a sister who was about to walk side by side with me during her pregnancy— and mine—if I was about to be blessed with such a gift. Christmas was only one week away, and I never felt more full of hope.

CHAPTER

Thirteen

The holidays arrived, and Wes and I took part in all the usual family festivities: turkey dinner at my parents' home on Christmas Eve, followed by a second meal at the Radcliffe mansion overlooking the sea at St. Margaret's Bay. We spent the night there, and woke up Christmas morning to open gifts with his family.

Sadly, it was not a white Christmas. It rained throughout the night, but that did not detract from the holiday merriment. There was much laughter and excitement as we dove into the presents and started ripping and tearing at the paper and gift bags.

That year, Barbara gave me a lovely jeweled pendant on a delicate gold chain—an oval-shaped emerald surrounded by diamonds, which must have cost a small fortune. She had purchased it in the Caribbean during one of their recent vacations, and she told me that she'd thought of me the moment she laid eyes on it. It was an exquisite piece, and I stood up to hug her in front of the tree.

I should mention that something had come up at the dinner table the night before: the question of when Wes and I were going to start a family.

"Will this be the year?" Barbara asked as she raised her wine glass to her lips and spoke with a twinkle in her eye.

Wes put his arm around me and pulled me close. He told her that we were working on it, and that we hoped to have some good news soon.

Everyone buzzed with delight and good wishes. It was a happy moment.

When Wes and I returned home in the evening on Christmas Day, the house was dark, and there were no outdoor lights to turn on because we just hadn't gotten around to stringing them up.

The temperature had dropped to below freezing, and it was an overcast night with no snow on the ground. We rushed inside, and the house was like an icebox. We removed our boots and gloves, turned on the heat, then flicked on some lights.

There were no toy helicopters to play with that night after we finished unpacking. All we did was sit on the sofa to watch CNN. Then we felt guilty for not making more of the fact that it was Christmas Day, so we watched *It's a Wonderful Life.*

When we went to bed, Wes apologized for being distant over the past few weeks, but he admitted that he'd felt smothered by all the pressure to conceive a child. He then confessed that he felt a weight had been lifted with the knowledge that it would make no difference if we made love during the crucial week of ovulation or not—or any other time for that matter. He told me he'd been suffering a bit of "performance anxiety" lately.

I felt terrible about that, and when he suggested that we take a break from sex until the new year, I agreed.

Despite what you might think, I did not feel rejected by

his request. In all honesty, I understood exactly where he was coming from, because I'd been putting a lot of pressure on myself as well—to light candles and wear sexy nighties and make sure "it" happened, whether or not we were in the mood.

I couldn't deny that I felt a sense of relief that he wanted to take a break, and start again in a week or two.

Also, it was the most intimate conversation we'd had in a long time. For months, I had been feeling as if we were growing more and more apart. We'd barely been communicating, but now, my husband was finally opening up to me and admitting his true feelings.

All I wanted, moving forward, was for us to feel connected again, and I believed, in that moment, that we had made progress.

I wished it could have been all roses and sunshine after that, but unfortunately, on the first day of school in early January, we came home at the end of the day and got into a terrible argument that started a snowball rolling.

Fourteen

In a way, I blame myself for how our fight started, because I had spent the holidays planning how and when we would begin IVF treatments with Dr. Walker—without ever talking to Wes about it.

In my defense, I had wanted to give him the time and space he needed and not put any more pressure on him. For that reason, I didn't mention my hopes, dreams and plans until after we returned to work in the New Year.

As it happened, for reasons of his own, Wes had decided not to bring up our fertility treatments during the holidays either. We simply didn't talk about it. We just tried to have a good time and be like a normal married couple.

We went out dancing with Scott and Angie on New Year's Eve, and drank lots of Champagne. We had a blast and I thought everything was on the upswing. I was simply biding my time until Wes and I could dive into the IVF treatments, full throttle.

I understand now that I had allowed myself to be blind—perhaps because the element of communication I had desired in our relationship was nowhere to be found. We were both maintaining a façade. We were pretending to be happy, and I didn't realize that each of us was keeping our true, honest thoughts and feelings to ourselves. The "disconnect" between us was deeper than ever.

_@_

"I'm not going to ask my parents for money again," Wes said as he stormed out of the kitchen and into the living room.

"But they have so much of it," I replied, finding it ridiculous that he was resisting the idea. "Your parents want us to have children as much as we do. I'm sure they would be happy to help us out. Remember when your mom gave me your sterling silver baby cup last Christmas? I'm certain she'll be totally on board. She'll be thrilled that we came to her and disappointed if we don't. Seriously, Wes, it would be pocket change to them."

He shot me a heated look. "The fact that they have money to spare is not the point."

"What *is* the point, then?" I asked. "Because I thought it was us having a child. I'm willing to do anything to make that happen. Aren't you?"

He whirled around to face me. "The point is, Claire, that when I was young, my father pushed me to go to law school or medical school or whatever. He just wanted me to do something he could brag about—and I resisted just to spite him, and he knew it." Wes threw up his hands. "I actually would have enjoyed law school, but I couldn't bring myself to follow his advice or do what he told me to do. I was determined to prove that I had a mind of my own, and I *wanted* to disappoint him. It gave me great satisfaction."

My head drew back in disbelief as I followed Wes from

the living room to the bedroom, because I couldn't see how his career choice and teenage conflicts with his father had anything to do with our struggles to have a child *today*.

"He was always controlling," Wes continued, "and you don't know how much pleasure he'll take when we go to him asking for money. He'll finally be able to say, 'See? You should have listened to me, boy. If you had done more with your life, you'd be able to afford this on your own.'"

Wes strode to the closet and rifled through his shirts and jackets. I knew what he was looking for. Even though it was early January, he wanted to go for a late-night run over jagged ice and snow in sub-zero temperatures.

He found a running jacket and slipped it on, over his head.

"So it's your pride that's stopping you," I said.

Wes glared at me for not backing off when perhaps I should have.

"Here's the truth, Claire," he said. "The cold hard truth, so you might want to brace yourself. None of this would be happening if you hadn't fallen off that stupid horse when you were fourteen." He exhaled sharply. "Fast forward almost twenty years. Now we need expensive medical treatments to fix your problem. But it's not *my* problem! I'm fine. I can have a kid whenever I damn well please—for *free*!" He shook his head at me. "I'm not going to let you drag me into a bottomless pit of debt, and humiliate me in front of my family. I'm not going to ask my father to give me money to pay for IVF, and that's that."

I followed him to the front door. "Then we can just get a line of credit," I suggested. "Or take a second mortgage on the house. He wouldn't even have to know. We'd just show up one day and tell them that we're pregnant. Easy as pie."

Wes sat down on the bench by the front door to pull on his sneakers. "You *would* say something like that. But nothing's easy about this. And you're missing the point again."

"Am I?" I felt a sudden rush of anger. "I don't think so. And I have news for you, Wes. Life is tough, and sometimes things don't work out exactly the way you want them to. Sometimes you get pushed down a hill, but you adapt, and you figure out a way to get what you want, even if it means making a few sacrifices."

I paused as he stood up and dug through the front hall basket for a baseball cap.

"Honestly, I don't care how we make it happen," I added. "I'd be perfectly willing to adopt a child if you don't want to pay for IVF. I just want to have a child with you and go back to being happy."

Wes glared at me. "It would take years to adopt, Claire. And you know I've always wanted to have lots of kids. If we have to pay a fortune every time, we'll be in debt up to our eyeballs. Besides, I'm not raising someone *else's* kid."

I blinked at him in disbelief. "It would be our child, and we would love him or her, no matter what."

"Speak for yourself." Wes whipped open the front door, went outside into the cold winter night, and jogged down the front steps. He stopped on the shoveled walk and turned to face me.

"I *do* want a kid of my own," he said harshly, looking up at me under the bluish, foggy light of the fluorescent porch lamp. "But I don't want to spend a fortune on IVF when I'm not even sure I want to start a family with *you*, Claire."

I stood frozen, stunned and beginning to shake. "What do you mean?"

He spread his gloved hands wide. "Look, I've already said it. Don't make me say it again." He began to jog on the spot, his breaths puffing out of his mouth like little bursts of smoke. I felt sick to my stomach.

"I think we both need to accept it," he added. "This isn't what we thought it would be, so maybe we should just cut our losses and go our separate ways before we waste any more time or energy trying to make this work—because you're not what I want."

I shivered in the cold air as my once-loving husband turned and jogged away from me, down the dark, snow-covered street. Then I went inside and sat down on the sofa in a numb and sickening state of shock.

CHAPTER

Fifteen

Feeling desperate, I tried calling Angie at home, but there was no answer. I then tried her cell phone, and thankfully she answered.

"Hey Claire, what's up?"

By this time, I was pacing back and forth in my kitchen, feeling lightheaded as I raked my fingers through my hair.

"You're not going to believe what just happened. Wes and I had a terrible fight. I can't believe the things he just said to me."

"What did he say?"

I shut my eyes, not even sure I could repeat the words without falling apart completely. Swallowing hard, I steeled myself. "He said he didn't want to pay for IVF, and that he didn't think he even wanted to have children with me at all."

There was a long silence. "Oh my God, Claire. Where are you?"

"I'm at home. He just went for a run. Where are you?"

"I'm at The Bicycle Thief having dinner with Scott. But do you want me to come over?"

"No, it's okay," I replied, not wanting to spoil their evening. "I just need to talk to someone. I'm in shock. I can't believe he said those things, and that he feels that way. I mean…I knew we were having some problems, but I didn't think it was *that* bad."

"I don't blame you," she replied. "And I can't believe it either. Everything seemed fine on New Year's Eve."

I continued to pace. "I don't know what to do, Angie. I don't want my marriage to end. I still love him, and I always imagined that he'd be the father of my children. I don't understand this. How could he just turn on a dime? It was so sudden. It came out of nowhere. This time last year, everything was perfect. We were so in love."

She was quiet for a moment. "Tell me again… What started the fight?"

"I brought up IVF and suggested that we ask his parents to help us pay for it, and that's what set him off. He didn't want to ask them for money, and it's complicated because he has some issues with his dad. I suggested that we get a line of credit and pay for it ourselves, but he refused that, too. He said the most awful things to me… That it wasn't his problem that I fell off a horse, and that he could have a child anytime he wanted, for free—so basically…why should he have to pay a fortune to have one with me?"

I couldn't hold it in any longer. I sank onto a kitchen chair, covered my face with my hand, and quietly wept while I held the phone a distance away, so that Angie wouldn't hear me.

"I should come over," she said. "Really, it's no problem. Scott will understand. He can bring me a doggy bag."

I pulled myself together and managed to speak without falling apart all over again.

"No, stay there and finish your dinner, because Wes usually only runs for half an hour when it's cold outside.

He'll probably be back soon, and maybe he'll regret what he said. Either way, we're going to need to talk this through."

"Okay," Angie said, "but call if you need me. And Claire, everything's going to be fine. He loves you. This is just a hiccup. All marriages have them. Scott and I have had our share. I'm sure Wes will walk in the door any minute, fall at your feet, and apologize for everything."

I wiped my cheek. "I don't know. This feels like more than a hiccup. But thanks Angie."

She was quiet for a moment, and I found myself listening in a stupor to the sounds of the restaurant—the music, the clinking of silverware, and the laughter of people at a nearby table. I wished I was among them, that Wes and I were together, enjoying a night out instead of fighting about money and our marriage, and my infertility.

I hung up the phone and went into the bathroom to blow my nose and clean up my face, because I'd made a mess of myself, crying so hard in the kitchen.

Then I poured myself a glass of wine and went into the living room to wait for Wes to return—all the while praying that Angie was right, and that my husband would walk through the door any minute and apologize for what he had said.

I sat down, and waited.

Sixteen

Wes did not come home after we fought that night. Instead, he ran to a friend's house—a former teacher at the school whom I had never met. At least Wes texted me to let me know where he was, because I grew worried after an hour when he didn't come home. It was below freezing outside.

In the text, he briefly apologized for his behavior, but said he needed some space.

I had no more tears left to shed at that point and felt almost dead inside. At the same time, anger was starting to boil in my veins. I texted him back and said, "Fine. Let's talk tomorrow."

I texted Angie to let her know that he hadn't come home and he was staying with a friend. Despite my objections, she came straight home from the restaurant and knocked on my door with her overnight bag.

"In the mood for a sleepover?" she asked, holding up a bottle of bourbon.

I laughed miserably and invited her in.

We got into our pajamas and stayed up until past midnight. She slept in Wes's spot in our bedroom and handed me tissues when I cried, and told me about all the terrible arguments she and Scott had had over the years, and how they'd always come back to each other with regret, their love stronger than before.

The following morning, she cooked breakfast for me and drove me to school, where I knew I would see Wes.

Angie told me to be strong and not to give up.

"He loves you," she said. "He just needs time to realize that, and to think about what he'd be giving up if he lost you. I'm sure he hasn't really considered the reality of living without you. When he does, he'll be back, and everything will be fine."

I thanked her and hugged her, then I got out of her car and walked into the school.

Imagine my surprise when I learned that Wes had called in sick and there was a substitute teacher in his place, running drills with the sixth graders.

As I backed out of the gymnasium—where I had gone searching for him, hoping to gain some clarity—I felt sick to my stomach all over again. I was so angry with him for his cowardice, because obviously, he was afraid to face me.

As the day progressed, it became more and more clear to me that Wes would not be coming home to grovel for my forgiveness. I couldn't help but read the writing on the wall: My husband didn't love me anymore, and my marriage might already be over.

How foolish and blind I had been over the holidays, believing it was the best Christmas ever, and that hope had been restored. I had truly believed that this would be the year we would make a baby, and that next Christmas would be our first, as new parents.

Now my sister—who wasn't even married or in a committed relationship—was pregnant, and all I saw in my immediate future was continued frustration, loneliness and heartbreak—and a very painful divorce from the man I still loved.

Things only got worse when I arrived home that night to an empty house. There were still no messages from Wes. I tried calling his cell because I wanted to face this head on and find out where we stood.

Was it truly over, or was there still a chance he might come around? I loved him and I wanted my marriage to work. Maybe he just needed some time. And I would have been perfectly willing to go to marriage counseling if he would agree to it. But he refused to answer my calls. They went straight to voicemail, as if he had turned off his phone.

Eventually, I called the friend who had offered his sofa to Wes the night before—which took some detective work on my part, because I didn't have the guy's phone number. All I knew was that his first name was Dave. Thankfully, one of my colleagues at school was able to help me.

At least Dave had the courage to answer his phone, but he was cryptic and sounded uneasy talking to me, as if I were asking him to betray Wes's confidence. I didn't know how much of it was true, but Dave informed me that Wes was not there, and that he had no idea where he had gone.

I thought about calling Bev, but I decided to call Angie instead because she had become something of a marriage counselor for me, always willing to listen and offer insight and advice, because she understood the effects of infertility on a marriage.

First I tried calling her cell, but she didn't answer, so I called her at home.

It was Scott who picked up the phone after a number of rings. His tone was not friendly.

CHAPTER

Seventeen

"Hi Scott," I said, feeling instantly ill at ease. "Is Angie there?"

There was a long pause. "No, she's not here."

I cleared my throat and wondered if I had interrupted him in the middle of something. "Do you know when she'll be back? I tried calling her cell just now, but she didn't answer."

Again, he paused, and my heart began to pound heavily with dread.

At last he spoke, more gently this time. "Are you at home right now, Claire?"

Feelings of angst and apprehension came at me from all angles, but I didn't understand why. I suppose some basic instinct was warning me that something was terribly, terribly wrong.

"Yes," I replied.

"Then you should probably come over here. Or I should come over there."

I blinked a few times and glanced around at the magazine clutter on the kitchen table and the dirty dishes in the sink, both of which I was in no mood to deal with.

"I'll come over there," I said. "Right now?"

"Yes," he replied. "I'll be here."

We ended the call, and I covered my face with both hands because I knew something must have happened.

Five minutes later, I rang his doorbell.

"Come in," Scott said as he stepped aside and invited me in.

He was dressed in a light blue linen shirt, untucked over faded blue jeans and Birkenstocks—which he wore almost every day of the year, even when it was below freezing outside.

He took my coat and invited me into the living room, where I noticed a half-empty bottle of red wine on the coffee table and a single glass.

"Let me pour you one," he said, taking note of the fact that I had fixed my eyes on it.

I didn't argue.

While he moved into the kitchen to fetch a glass, I sat down on the white leather sofa. He didn't speak as he returned and poured my wine. He handed it to me, and I accepted it.

"When you called," he said, "I thought you wanted to talk to Angie about Wes."

Scott sat down on the opposite end of the sofa and rested his elbows on his knees. He wove his fingers together while he waited for me to respond.

I took a giant gulp of the wine, set it down on the coffee table, and nodded. "She probably told you about all my marriage woes. I'm sorry, Scott. I'm embarrassed, and I apologize for spoiling your dinner last night. You must have been annoyed with me for stealing Angie away all night."

He bowed his head and shook it. "Don't be embarrassed, Claire. And I wasn't annoyed."

I sucked in a breath and let it out, while waiting for him to explain why he had invited me over. Finally, his eyes lifted.

"I don't know how to tell you this," he said, "but Wes and Angie are on their way to Toronto right now."

I sat back, as if he'd swung a punch at me. "I beg your pardon?"

Scott bowed his head again and squeezed his hands together. "This is difficult." He didn't look at me this time. "There's no easy way to put this. Your husband and my wife have run off together. They've been having an affair since the fall."

A hot fireball of anxiety exploded in my stomach, and I immediately launched into a position of denial. "That can't be true."

"I wish it weren't."

I stared at him in horror and stood up quickly. "That's insane, Scott. If my husband was sleeping with another woman—*my best friend*—I would have suspected something."

I stormed out from behind the coffee table to the space on the white shag carpet, directly in front of the stone fireplace, where I paced back and forth.

Just last night, Angie had come to my door offering comfort and a shoulder to cry on, and she had encouraged me not to lose hope.

He loves you, she had said, many times. *Everything will be fine…*

Was she that good of an actress?

No, it couldn't be true.

"What in the world would make you think something like that?" I asked Scott. "Do you have any proof? And are you sure Wes is with her? He never mentioned anything to me, and he wouldn't just leave the province without a single word. He never even packed a bag."

Scott watched me with a look of sympathy and pity, which made me want to scream.

"Angie called me from New Brunswick to tell me what was happening," he explained.

"When?"

"An hour ago. They took the Audi."

I stared at him with wide eyes. "And you're *sure* Wes was with her? She actually said that?"

Oh God... Maybe Wes *had* packed a bag. I hadn't checked the closet where we keep our suitcases, or his drawers. He could have packed it days ago and removed it from the house when I wasn't at home.

Scott nodded, and I paced some more.

"She spent the night at my house last night," I argued. "She stayed up with me, watching me cry over Wes, handing me tissues and telling me everything was going to be okay. She was such a good friend to me. I can't believe she could be *that* deceiving. That much of a backstabber."

"If it makes you feel any better," Scott said, "I had no idea what was coming either. When I took her out to dinner last night, I was hoping we could figure out a way to save our marriage, and yours as well."

"So you knew about this since the fall?"

He shook his head. "Not for sure. I only suspected it, until New Year's Eve when I sensed they were hiding something. Couldn't you see it? There was an energy between them. I hadn't seen Angie act like that since we first started dating, years ago."

By now, my stomach was turning somersaults. I returned to the sofa, sat down, and gulped down the rest of my wine to try and calm my nerves.

"I didn't notice anything on New Year's Eve," I said. "But if what you're saying is true…what is wrong with me? How could I be that blind?" Scott said nothing, while I squeezed at my hair. "I was so consumed with wanting to have a baby with him. This is all my fault. I've been completely self-absorbed."

"Don't blame yourself," Scott said in a low, husky voice that contained a hint of bitterness. "They hid it well."

"Not from *you*." I poured more wine. "But let's back up a bit. If you knew this on New Year's Eve, why didn't you tell me?"

"Because I didn't feel we knew each other well enough, and I kind of thought you *did* know…that you must. And the whole time, I kept hoping that it was just a momentary weakness, for both of them, and they'd eventually realize their mistake and put an end to it."

"Would you have forgiven her?"

"I don't know," he replied, looking down at the floor. "I just didn't want my marriage to go up in flames."

I felt sick to my stomach and stood up. "I'm sorry… I have to use the bathroom."

I hurried to the powder room off the kitchen, got down on my knees, raised the lid and waited for the contents of my stomach to come up, but it didn't happen. All I could do was stare into the toilet bowl, imagining my husband in my best friend's SUV, holding her hand and feeling grateful to have escaped without being found out—without ever having to face his wife and admit his infidelity.

When did he intend to tell me? When he arrived in Toronto, knowing that he'd made a clean getaway? Or weeks later, when I thought he might be lying in a ditch somewhere, frozen and dead?

I imagined myself calling the police to file a missing person's report, then being humiliated when they located him at some sleazy hotel, having run off with another woman.

I leaned forward, wanting to vomit—but again, I couldn't. I even stuck my finger down my throat, trying desperately to expel everything, but nothing worked, and I still felt nauseous.

Falling onto my behind and inching away from the toilet to sit back against the door, I shut my eyes and hugged my knees to my chest. The despair that churned in my gut was unbearable. It was far worse than all the monthly disappointments over the past year, each time my period started and I had to accept that I wasn't pregnant. This was different, because my husband had left me. I had to face the fact that he loved another woman.

My heart squeezed painfully in my chest as I realized that I hadn't been enough for him. He had preferred someone else. He had been sexually attracted to Angie, probably since the first moment we all met.

*Oh, God...*when I had spoken my vows at the altar, I had trusted him wholeheartedly and believed our love for each other was everlasting and indestructible. Mine certainly had been. But he didn't want to be with me anymore. He didn't care that he was hurting me in this way. He had no concept or concern for the pain I was feeling. He wanted nothing more to do with me. He was gone.

I began to shake uncontrollably. All the happiness I had let into my life was annihilated. We were never going to have a baby together, nor would we ever be a happy family—not after this. All my dreams for a happy future with the man I loved were blowing apart in front of my eyes and I was in shock, just like that day when I was twelve and my mother told me my father was dead.

Now, I was not only infertile, but heartbroken and rejected by the man I trusted. The only thing ahead of me was anguish and heartache while I struggled to accept what Wes had done to us.

And Angie—the female friend I had also trusted completely—had betrayed me as well, in the most hurtful, deceitful, and calculating way.

She knew how upset I was about the possible breakdown of my marriage. I had confided in her about everything, even the death of my father. Yet she took advantage of my trust and stole my husband away, knowing exactly where the cracks were in my marriage, and where she could begin to dig in.

How long had she been planning it? Since the moment we walked through her door a year ago with a plate of cookies? Or since I told her that Wes had excellent sperm motility, when her own husband had problems in that area?

Was that why she'd wanted my husband?

Heaven help me... My thoughts were running amuck. Of course that couldn't have been it. If Angie just wanted sperm, she and Scott could have found a donor ages ago. This was something else—an attraction I hadn't recognized.

A knock sounded at the bathroom door.

"Claire, are you okay?" Scott asked.

I rose to my feet and opened the door. "Yes. I was just having a bit of a nervous breakdown."

He looked at me with compassion. "I'm sorry. I wish this wasn't happening."

"Me, too. But thank you for telling me. At least now I know."

I flicked off the bathroom light and returned to the living room where I stood in a daze, staring blankly at the empty grate in the fireplace. I couldn't seem to move. My body felt like lead.

"Would you like another glass of wine?" Scott asked. "Or something stronger?" He glanced toward the liquor cabinet.

I closed my eyes and exhaled. "No, I should probably go. I need to call my sister and tell her about this, and figure out what I'm going to do. I really have no idea. I have no bearings."

It seemed impossible to accept the reality that my husband was with Angie at that very moment.

What were they talking about? Were they making plans for the future? Talking about what a fool I was?

Oh, God…

What if Angie was pregnant? What if *that's* why they ran off together?

My stomach muscles clenched tight with jealousy and humiliation. I felt utterly defeated—a failure as a wife and a woman.

"Do you know where they'll be staying?" I asked.

Scott shook his head. "Probably a hotel on the road. When they arrive in Toronto… I don't know."

Feeling queasy again, I walked to the door and pulled on

my boots while Scott retrieved my coat from the closet. Neither of us spoke as he held up my parka and I slid my arms into the sleeves, then zipped it up.

"Thank you for being honest with me," I finally said. "Delivering that news couldn't have been easy."

"None of this has been easy," he replied.

I nodded and turned to go, because there was nothing more to say, and I was completely drained.

"I'm sorry, Claire," Scott said as I walked down the front steps.

"I'm sorry, too," I replied.

I jogged across the street and walked through the door of my empty house. For a moment I stood motionless in my coat and boots, staring into space, listening to the clock ticking on the wall.

I turned my gaze to the spot in the corner where the Christmas tree had stood not long ago. I remembered how full of hope I had been when I finished decorating it and plugged in the lights. The whole room had seemed to light up with magic.

This is going to be a wonderful year, I had thought, as I stood back to admire it. *By next Christmas, we might be parents…*

What a fool I was.

Swallowing over the grief that rose up in my throat, I removed my coat and finally picked up the phone to call Bev.

CHAPTER

Eighteen

A week later, I was more of a wreck than I had been the night Scott told me about my husband's affair. I suppose it had taken that long for it to fully sink in, even after the school principal advised me that Wes had handed in his resignation the day before he left. I couldn't believe no one at work had mentioned anything to me. I suppose they thought I knew.

At first, I was in a state of denial, believing that Wes would wake up from this insanity, realize he'd made a terrible mistake, and come home. Then we would be able to pick up the pieces and begin to repair our marriage.

When he finally did contact me, he did so by text, which had been especially cruel because that didn't give me a chance to vent my anger or ask any questions.

Was he ever coming back? What about our house? I couldn't afford the mortgage payments on my own. Did his parents know?

But he continued to ignore my calls. All he said in the text message was this:

You probably know where I am by now, and I'm sorry for blindsiding you like this, but I thought it would be better than dragging things out. There was no way for either Angie or me to make this easy on you, or to let you down gently. It was going to be painful no matter what, so I think this is the best way—to avoid a scene—then we can all move on.

I was so shocked and angered by his text, I began to hyperventilate in my kitchen while fighting the temptation to smash my phone against the wall.

Then he sent a second message:

But it can't be a total shock to you, Claire. You knew I wasn't happy. For that reason, I think a clean break is better for everyone because I'm not going to change my mind. Please stop trying to contact me. It'll only make things harder on you and me both. Again, I'm sorry. You're a good person, Claire, and I feel terrible about all of this. I know it wasn't your fault that you fell off that horse. But I'm not coming home. I just need to move on. We'll need to get a divorce. Let's just get this over with, without any drama. You should probably get a lawyer.

My blood pressure hit the roof. I'm lucky I didn't have a stroke right there, because the way he was messaging me—as if I were being unreasonable for trying to contact him—made me lose control.

My cheeks burned and I gritted my teeth until my jaw ached. I let out a deep, guttural scream and finally threw my cell phone against the wall.

By some miracle it didn't break, thanks to the protective pink rubber case that Wes had bought me for Christmas. Had he *known* I was going to throw it against the wall a month later?

Heart racing, blood pounding in my ears like thunder, I stared at my phone on the floor. I thought about what Wes had done. Then I marched over, picked it up, ripped off the garish pink protector, and smashed the phone repeatedly on the kitchen table top, wishing it was his stupid, selfish head.

I broke the screen and felt satisfied at last. But only for a few seconds, then I burst into tears and collapsed on a chair.

My brain was functioning at hyper-speed. Thoughts were bouncing around inside my head like rubber balls. I quickly typed a message through my tears and the broken glass: *Just tell me this. Is she pregnant? Is that why you left with her?*

He responded immediately: *No, she's not pregnant. We just need to be together. You wouldn't understand. I'm turning off my phone now.*

I stared at his message with disbelief. He thinks I wouldn't understand? Does he believe I have no concept of love or passion, or how charismatic Angie could be?

It was a low moment, one of many during those first few weeks. I could barely remember half of them. I just remember the anger and the tears.

One bright spot was my sister Bev, who was constantly supportive and sympathetic. As soon as I called her that first night, she had come over with Leo and never left. She moved in temporarily, so that I wouldn't have to be alone while I came to terms with the situation.

I was grateful for her presence, especially at night when fantasies about my future were bleak and pathetic. I imagined myself as the forever lonely, barren wife whose husband left her for another more beautiful woman who could give him a child.

I had other fantasies, too, where I confronted Angie and told her how cruel she had been, and how much pain she had caused. I told her I would never forgive her, not as long as I lived, because she was a wicked, rotten husband-stealer who deserved a lifetime of karmic unhappiness.

I wanted her to feel pain, too—to regret her actions, and to suffer with excruciating guilt, and never escape the shame over what she had done to me.

Looking back on it, I realize that my anger only caused me more intense levels of suffering. Had I simply accepted it and "moved on," as Wes had suggested, I might have spared myself a lot of heartache and rage. But I simply had to go through that firestorm. I had to let it run its course. Only then, could I recover and let it go.

But I wasn't there yet. Even after a month, I was still heartbroken and pathetic.

And Bev, now almost twenty-weeks pregnant, was still living with me.

When her apartment lease came up for renewal a week later, I asked her to move in with me permanently, because she would no doubt need help with her baby when the time came.

She was hesitant because she didn't want to be a burden, but I wanted to be there for my sister, just as she had always been there for me. And I think, deep down, I wanted the opportunity to bond with her baby, and be a good auntie, because I feared it might be my only chance to have a child in my life.

"I just want my husband back," I confessed to Bev one evening as we sat on the sofa re-watching a first-season episode of *Downton Abbey*. "I keep dreaming that he'll show up at the door and tell me how sorry he is, and that he made a terrible mistake and he still loves me, and that Angie could never take my place. Then I imagine how upset and heartbroken she would be when he left her. She'd throw a tantrum and be miserable in Toronto. She'd die alone with a bunch of cats."

"Sounds like quite a revenge fantasy." Bev raised the remote control and paused the episode. "But seriously, Claire? You'd take Wes back after what he did to you?"

I buried my forehead in my hand and groaned. "Oh, I don't know. I just want him to come back and grovel, and I want Angie to get what she deserves."

"If he actually did that," Bev said, still pressing me, "would you really take him back?"

I thought about it for a moment. "Part of me would love to kick him to the curb, just to give him a taste of his own medicine. But he's my husband. We're not the first couple to go through something like this, you know. Infidelity happens. That doesn't make it right, but good people sometimes make mistakes, and some couples make it through and come out of it even stronger on the other end."

Bev said nothing. She simply watched me while I continued to ramble, working through my feelings, trying to rationalize what I wanted.

"I just always imagined that Wes and I would grow old together," I explained. "And remember… We were under a lot of pressure over the past year. Most of it was my fault because of the infertility issues. I was the one pushing us to see a doctor and to have sex every time I was ovulating. But doesn't everyone deserve a second chance? And forgiveness?"

"You always did have a forgiving nature," Bev replied. "You don't hold grudges. You didn't even hold one against Shelly Cartwright in the sixth grade, when she elbowed you in the parade, just as you were about to throw your baton. She made you drop it, then she threw hers and got all the applause. You cried your eyes out that night and said you'd hate her forever."

"I did hate her for a while," I said, "but then we ended up being really good friends in high school. I figured that we were just kids back then. She'd matured."

Bev raised an eyebrow. "You're a better woman than I am—because I still hated her, even years later, when you were besties."

I inclined my head. "Are you saying that if I took Wes back, you'd always hate him?"

Bev stood up and went to the kitchen to fill Leo's food bowl. He followed and began crunching on his dinner.

"I don't know," Bev replied. "Maybe. I guess I'm just not as forgiving as you." She returned and sat back down. "But it doesn't matter how I feel. It's your life. But think about it this way. I admire your desire to forgive. I think it's very honorable. But maybe you can forgive him without actually taking him back. You can just bury the hatchet, let your ego wallow in the pleasure of knowing that he regretted it, but then move on without bitterness, and find someone else who would never dream of being unfaithful to you, or hurting you like that."

I rested my arm along the back of the sofa. "You don't think people can change? Or learn and grow from their mistakes?"

She gazed out the dark window for a moment. "I do think people learn from their mistakes, but certain mistakes take too great a toll on others, and I think the offender's lesson should be the loss of what they didn't value enough. Then they *really* learn something."

"So you think that if I took him back, I'd be depriving him of the lesson he needs to learn?"

"Yes," she said firmly. "That's exactly what I think." She sipped her water and shook her head at herself. "Although…I do believe in second chances, just not in Wes's case. Not after the way he handled everything—first, letting the affair happen, and then just leaving without ever talking to you about it, and sending those awful, heartless texts. It was selfish and mean, and conniving. What does that say about what's inside his core?"

"He is an ass," I finally agreed. "But at least he's still paying his half of the mortgage. It comes out of his bank account every two weeks and so far, he hasn't stopped those payments. Thank God for that, because he knows I can't afford it on my own."

Bev raised an eyebrow. "I hate to be the pessimist here, but I doubt it's out of the goodness of his heart. He's probably still paying it because he intends to claim his half of this house in the divorce. You may be in for a fight there."

I sighed with resignation. "You're probably right."

"Of course I am. So how would you ever be able to trust a person who could be so calculating and cruel? He didn't care about your feelings at all when he walked out. Is that the kind of man you want raising your children?"

While I considered all of that—and decided that *no*, he was not the man I wanted as a father figure to my children—Bev raised the remote control and pressed PLAY. Leo entered the living room and lay down on the floor at her feet.

I returned my attention to the television for a moment. Then I looked out the front window at Scott and Angie's house across the street. There was a light on in the living room, and the porch light was on as well, but I knew it was the timer because Scott was not at home.

He had left me a phone message a few days after he broke the news to me about Wes and Angie. He had called to let me know that he'd accepted a consulting assignment in Munich, and he was leaving right away.

"Not to sound like a cliché," he said in the voicemail, "but I'm going to throw myself into my work."

I had recognized the pain in his voice, and I understood why he was leaving. He needed to escape this nightmare.

Sometimes I wanted to escape it, too, and get out of this house where I was surrounded by all the things that Wes and I had bought together, and all the memories. It was impossible not to think of the betrayal, every single day.

I never called Scott back, but I had sent him an email to let him know I understood.

He emailed me back and asked if I would check on his house once a week to make sure no pipes had burst.

I agreed and he dropped off a key. I wished him well at my front door, and hadn't heard from him since.

CHAPTER

Nineteen

A nother month went by, and each new day was easier than the last. Eventually, I was able to let go of the fantasy that Wes would come crawling home to me and everything would go back to the way it was.

The catalyst for that particular change in me was the arrival of papers from his lawyer, declaring us legally separated. According to family law in Nova Scotia, we had to be separated for a year before we could file for divorce, and Scott wanted to make it official.

In an instant, I was wrenched out of my denial and thrust into a state of anger, where I decided there would *never* be any forgiveness for either of them. From that day forward, Wes and Angie were dead to me. I didn't want to waste another second of my life agonizing over what they were doing together. I made a pact with myself that I would no longer care. I hoped they would stay in Toronto, so that I would never have to lay eyes on either of them again.

I signed the papers.

A few days later, I received a brief email from Scott one evening when Bev was working the night shift at the hospital. He wanted to let me know that he, too, had received separation papers from Angie's lawyer. He just thought I should know.

I sat down at my laptop and typed a reply:

Dear Scott,

Thanks so much for the message. It's good to hear from you. I received separation papers as well, from Wes's lawyer in Toronto. I wonder if it's the same firm?

I told him the name of it, and with that, I realized I was not quite as "over it" as I wanted to be, and I still had some grumbling to do. I also still craved information about their affair, because I knew so little about it.

But at least I wasn't daydreaming about a marital reconciliation. That ship—thank goodness—had sailed.

I continued my message to Scott:

Your house is fine. I've checked it every week, and I changed the lightbulb in the living room where you have the timer set up, after it didn't come on one night. I'll continue to keep an eye on things until you return.

On that note, how is Germany? Are you drinking lots of German beer and doing the polka?

I signed off and pressed send.

Twenty minutes later, my email program chimed and I sat down with a hot cup of tea to read Scott's reply.

Dear Claire,

Yes, indeed, the papers from Angie came from the same firm. Obviously that means they are still together, which I suppose is no surprise. I've not heard from Angie at all. She wouldn't answer my calls at first, so

I just stopped trying because it became degrading after a while.

And Germany is good. The work keeps me occupied. I feel very far away from what happened, but I'm not sure if that's a good thing. Sometimes it doesn't seem real, and I imagine returning home, just like every other business trip, and Angie will pick me up at the airport and life will return to normal. It's hard to believe that my house is empty right now. I imagine it will feel very cold when I come back.

Also, I've been thinking about what happened, and I feel like I should apologize to you. First of all, I feel badly for not coming to you sooner with the information, and then for taking off and leaving you there to watch my house. All I wanted to do was escape the whole situation. But you've had to remain at your post, with the added chore of walking through my house once a week, to look at all of Angie's things—the furniture she picked out and the clothes she left behind—and no doubt remember how we had all been such good friends in that house. Sometimes I think of us playing board games on our coffee table and I can't believe what happened. But then I try not to think about it. I focus on work.

Anyway, I'm sorry for rambling on and on. I'll be back soon and I'll bring you something cool from Germany. I don't know what it will be yet. Is there anything you would like?

That's probably a strange question.

All for now,

Scott

I chuckled when I came to the end of his email, took a sip of my tea, then began to type my reply.

Hi again. You said you were coming home soon. Any idea when?

And it's really not necessary to bring me anything. I didn't mind watching your house. (But I can't lie. I did sometimes find it difficult to walk through there and revisit the good times we had, and to see

Angie's things. But it got easier after the first few times.)

Now that I think about it, I wouldn't say no to some European chocolates. Just sayin'.

Claire

PS. What time is it there? It's supper time here.

I surfed the web while I waited for his reply, although I stayed away from Facebook, because when Wes first left me, I had checked his page obsessively—again, craving information and answers. But neither he nor Angie had posted a single thing. No pictures, no status updates, nothing. It was as if they had both just dropped off the face of the earth.

Eventually I stopped checking, and it felt better to remove that angst from my life.

Scott replied five minutes later.

Hi again. I should be home in a few weeks, by the end of April at the latest. And we are 5 hours ahead of you, so it's 10 pm here.

S.

I had to admit I was disappointed that his reply was so brief and he didn't ask any more questions that required me to write another note. It seemed appropriate to end the conversation, and I needed to take Leo outside for a quick walk, so I sent one last message:

End of April. Cool. I will keep an eye on things here until then. Take care, and feel free to message me if you need a ride from the airport.

C.

I closed my laptop and walked away. It chimed as I was attaching Leo's leash to his collar, so I hurried back to check it.

Thanks Claire! I'll be in touch. And please take care of yourself. I know it's tough right now, but we'll get through this. You'll see.
S.

His words at the end were incredibly comforting, because they made me feel as if I weren't completely alone in this. I was not the only casualty of Wes and Angie's affair.

Bev, of course, had been phenomenal, but she didn't *truly* understand what I was going through, not like Scott did, because he was wounded, too. We were like two soldiers in the same trench who had been hit with shrapnel, and lived to tell about it. No one else in the world could ever truly understand what it was like. We were the only ones who knew.

I typed another reply while Leo waited patiently by the door, tail wagging:

Thank you, Scott. I really appreciate you saying that.
Talk soon,
C.

There were no more messages after that, but I slept a little better that night. I kept thinking of those final words: *We'll get through this. You'll see.*

For the first time, I believed that I would, and I began to accept that this was an end to one part of my life and the beginning of another. My future was unknown at this point, but at least there would be one, and surely it could only get better from here.

I knocked on wood with that thought.

Twenty

The following night around supper time, my laptop chimed again.

I hurried to the desk in the living room and opened it to discover another email from Scott.

Hi again. I just wanted to check in about that light bulb that went out in my living room. I couldn't help but wonder if you were able to find a replacement in my house somewhere, or if you had to buy one or use one of your own. We keep them in the cupboard over the sink in the laundry room, so if it happens again, that's where they are.

Please reply. I feel like a cliché again. I've been playing solitaire every night. Help.

Scott

I chuckled and sat down at the desk.

Hi. I'm here. I'm going to type you a longer message which might take a few minutes, but I wanted you to know it's coming. Sit tight. Play a couple more hands…

I pressed SEND, then I sat back and wondered what to write.

He was playing solitaire. I had played it, too, in the early days after Wes left, and I knew exactly how Scott felt. Even the name of the game was depressing. So I began to type...

Ah, Solitaire... My addiction and my savior for a while. I finally put a stop to it by going to the bookstore and browsing around one Sunday afternoon. I came home with an armful of books and I've been reading a lot since then. The good thing about reading a book is that you never feel guilty about the hours you spend on it, because when you finish, there's a sense of accomplishment. I always feel like I've put another intellectual notch in my belt. I highly recommend it as an alternative to computer games.

Claire

I hit SEND.
Scott's reply came in five minutes later.

Excellent advice. I used to be a huge reader, but I read less now because I'm always on my phone or laptop—which I do feel guilty about, because I end up reading news items or tweets, or watching cat videos, and there's no sense of accomplishment in that! You've inspired me. I will go to the bookstore tomorrow and see what I can find in the English language. So what books have you been reading lately? Can you recommend anything good?

Scott

This was getting fun, because I loved talking about books, so I had no problem discharging the next message:

Dear Scott,

I've been reading all sorts of things—fiction and non-fiction. I started with some of the recent monster bestsellers, just to see what all the fuss was about. I read Gone Girl *(very suspenseful and I recommend it if you haven't seen the movie, because it's better if you don't know the ending).* I found The Light Between Oceans *a bit slow to get going, but the second half was terrific and I couldn't put it down. I'd say the same thing about* Room. *I loved* The Girl on the Train, *but I had some friends who didn't care for it because the main female character is so flawed. But it was a fascinating read if you can accept her with all of her issues, forgive her, and just go along for her crazy ride. Then I read the entire Harry Potter series because I am embarrassed to say I'd never read it before. Now I feel like a whole person.*

For non-fiction, I read a few self-help books…Eckhart Tolle and Wayne Dyer. I needed that. I also read a new edition of Stephen Hawking's book A Brief History of Time *which appealed to my science and math background. It contained a lot of physics, but I feel smarter now and proud of myself for getting through it. And Malcolm Gladwell is great. Try* Outliers *and* The Tipping Point. *You'll really like those.*

Claire

Dear Claire,

Thanks for these. I've read Gladwell's articles in The New Yorker *and I've heard great things about his books. I will give them a try. I might skip* The Girl on the Train, *however, because I'm not feeling terribly forgiving right now about women with flaws. I think I'm going through an angry phase. Doing too much thinking lately about Angie and all her issues, which kind of defeats the purpose of leaving the country and coming to Munich. It seemed like a good idea at the time, but now I think I should have stayed and faced it all.*

S.

I read Scott's message and felt a bit stunned by his candor. Up until this point, he hadn't revealed much emotion to me, except for the initial apology for taking off and asking me to watch his house. Otherwise, he'd seemed to be handling it all pretty well—unlike me, who smashed cell phones and cried buckets of tears for weeks.

Although…maybe he had smashed a few cell phones, too. In private.

Dear Scott,

I understand. I'm still pretty angry, too. What's been the worst for me is not knowing any of the details of how this happened, and what started it, and when. It was such a shock when you told me they had run off together, and Wes was already gone so I couldn't ask him any questions or demand to know the truth, or just shout at him. Then he refused to take my calls, which I'm assuming was for legal reasons, so that I would have as little ammunition as possible for the divorce. I just feel like I'm in the dark here, and sometimes I'm overcome with jealousy when I imagine them together. And jealousy and anger seem to go hand in hand. For my own sanity, like you, I try not to think about it, but it's not easy when my imagination gets the better of me. Maybe if I knew the truth, I could stop inventing scenarios. What's that saying? Curiosity killed the cat? Maybe I just need to let go of the desire to know all the gory details. Maybe that would be even more painful.

Dear Claire,

The truth would definitely be painful, but I can't help but think it would be better to just grit our teeth and bear it, otherwise we'll remain in this limbo. I wish now that I hadn't taken this job. That I had gotten in the car and chased after Angie, and had it out with her. I would tell her how foolish she was being, to assume that the grass would be greener elsewhere. And I'd ask her what she was searching for that she couldn't find in our own marriage when I was the most forgiving and understanding husband on the face of the earth—although I have my suspicions. I'm like you. The suddenness of it all makes it hard to process.

S.

I sat back for a moment and chewed on my thumbnail. Adrenaline flared through my veins, and anger reared its head again—but not at Scott. His emails were like a cold drink of water after days of stumbling through the hot desert. I was devouring every word he wrote, and I wanted more.

I sat forward and began typing…

Did Angie ever tell you anything about their affair? You said you've been thinking about Angie's "issues" lately. May I ask what those issues are? Because one of the things I wish I knew was which one of them started it, and considering how she lied to me… Had Angie ever cheated on you before? Or lied to you?

I hit SEND, and waited. For a long moment, I sat there, staring at the computer screen, clicking the RECEIVE button repeatedly to check for a reply. Minutes passed by at a snail's pace, and still, Scott did not answer, so I finally stood up and went to the kitchen to make a cup of tea.

At last, my laptop chimed, and I rushed back to the desk with my mug.

Hi again Claire,

I don't believe Angie ever cheated on me in the past, but after this, I'll never really know. When we were first married, I used to travel a lot, which was a bone of contention between us, especially when she wanted to get pregnant and I was often away at the crucial time each month. It took us a long time to figure out that the problem wasn't just my absence, but my sperm count. (I'm assuming she told you that we had fertility issues; she told me about yours). That's what I meant when I said I had my suspicions. I can't help but wonder if she was attracted to Wes because he could give her something I couldn't.

S.

Dear Scott,

Please don't blame yourself. She could have suggested a sperm donor instead of stealing another woman's husband. Sorry, I'm still angry. But do you think she was the one who initiated it?

(To be honest, I've had similar thoughts... That Wes was attracted to Angie for the same reason—because she could give him something I couldn't. We are two very different peas in a pod!)

Dear Claire,

Yes, indeed, we are. And I wish I knew who initiated it, but I don't. It could just as easily have been Wes, considering the issues you guys were having. Sorry, Claire, I don't mean to be hurtful, but I think we need to be honest with ourselves. They were probably both frustrated with us, and that's what started the intimacies and private conversations. They felt a need to commiserate.

But that doesn't excuse it. I'm just trying to put the puzzle pieces together. But truthfully...if I had to guess, I would bet it was Angie who started the conversations. She's very good at getting people to open up to her, which is part of her appeal. The problem is that she uses that ability to get what she wants. She can be a brilliant manipulator.

You'd think, after years of marriage, I would have been able to recognize it better. Sometimes I did, but not always, especially when I was on the receiving end of it.

S.

Reading those words made me feel sad for Scott, but at the same time, it was like a balm to my heart—to know that I was not alone in my anger toward Angie and her lack of integrity, and how she had manipulated me and charmed Wes.

It felt good to hear these criticisms of her, yet I didn't want to be the kind of woman who enjoys fueling her own hatred and negativity. Deep down, I wanted to forgive both of them so that I could let go of all the toxic jealousy and bitterness inside of me. I had come a long way, but it was impossible to completely forgive without a deeper understanding of Angie's so-called issues. And Wes's as well.

I took a moment to gather my thoughts, then I began typing again.

You're not being hurtful. I appreciate your honesty, and it's not like I haven't come to that conclusion myself—that Wes wanted a woman who could give him a child. It just pisses me off, because Wes and I had options. We were about to start IVF treatments, and I believe we could have been successful with that, if he hadn't thrown in the towel so soon.

C.

He might not have thrown in the towel if Angie hadn't been there to encourage him in that direction. I'm sorry, Claire. I'm sorry we moved in across the street from you. If we hadn't, your marriage might still be intact.

S.

I sat back and felt a heavy pang in my heart for Scott and the guilt he should not be feeling.

Please, Scott. It's not your fault. And I'm not sorry—because I'm glad I found out what kind of man Wes really was deep down. I just can't believe I never knew the real him. I thought I was marrying a man with a stronger sense of commitment and deeper family values, but obviously, my love was blind.
    C.

Dear Claire,
    Don't beat yourself up about it. You're a trusting person who believes in people. If it makes you feel any better, my love was blind, too. Although, I think I always knew Angie was impulsive and selfish. But I married her anyway. There was just something about her that was irresistible. Not only was she drop dead gorgeous, she had a spark when we first met—like no other woman I'd ever known, but unfortunately for me, it didn't last long after we were married. I suspect that's what's in store for Wes. It was that spark and excitement that he found attractive. But he'll soon realize his mistake when Angie's needy, unhappy personality emerges. It won't be long before the excitement of their affair wears off, and then I suspect Angie will get bored with Wes—especially if there's no money—and make his life miserable. I think he'll look back on his marriage to you and regret ever having left you, Claire. Because you're a sensible, good woman. He has no idea how lucky he was.
    S.

Those last words made my eyes fill with tears, and I felt a flicker of happiness, to know that I was not completely undesirable. Someone thought I was worth something.

I wiped my cheek and slowly typed my reply.

Thank you, Scott. I appreciate that more than you can ever know.
C.

I hit SEND, and waited for his response. It took awhile, but I was more patient this time.

Dear Claire,

If it helps you to know, Angie was always jealous of you. She said you were the kindest person she'd ever met, and that it wasn't fair that someone like you couldn't be a mother, when someone like her could. She actually said those words to me just before Christmas. I think at that point, she was already planning to take Wes away from you, and some decent part of her was ashamed. Didn't stop her from doing it, though.

As for her "issues" and why she is the way she is… She had a rough childhood. Both her parents were alcoholics and her father took off when she was in her teens. They've been estranged ever since. She hasn't seen him or spoken to him in over a decade, and her mother passed away from breast cancer a number of years ago, so Angie's been on her own. She has a brother, but he's not someone she can rely on. He has addiction problems as well and he lives in Texas now.

I guess that's why I've always been so forgiving with her—because I know she has a hard time believing that people can actually be dependable. I think that's why she likes to latch on to new people. She likes to accumulate friends, in case others disappear.
S.

By now, I had tears streaming down my cheeks. This was so disheartening to hear, and I genuinely felt sorry for Angie. But it was also cathartic, to know the truth. I took a deep breath and typed my reply.

Dear Scott,

Thank you for all this. Talking to you about it has really helped. It has given me a great deal of clarity. I don't feel quite so in the dark anymore.

C.

Dear Claire,

I feel better, too—getting all that off my chest and explaining Angie to you. Now I should probably get some sleep. It's past midnight here and I have to be up at six for a meeting in Salzburg. I'm looking forward to the train ride. It should be beautiful.

S.

Salzburg! I envy you. I've always wanted to visit Austria. How long will you be there?

C.

A couple of days. I have to educate the local IT team on the new systems.

S.

I imagined him getting on the train in the morning, passing through old European towns and approaching the Alps. What an adventure. I responded with:

I did some research on that part of Europe when Wes and I were booking our honeymoon. Did you know there's a Sound of Music *tour in Salzburg? Just google it if you're interested, and if you go, take some pictures. I'd love to hear all about it.*

C.

Thanks Claire. I love The Sound of Music. *It was a family tradition at my house—to watch it every Christmas when we were kids. Happy memories. I'll definitely look that up.*

Goodnight, Claire. I'll email you again soon.

S.

I sent him a quick reply to say goodnight, and felt a great weight lift from my shoulders as I let out a breath and closed my laptop. Then I took Leo for a quick walk. It was a beautiful night.

CHAPTER

Twenty-one

Scott and I continued to email each other every night for the next three weeks. Eventually, we stopped talking about our spouses and their affair. He took *The Sound of Music* tour in Salzburg and emailed me pictures, which I greatly enjoyed.

We also discussed the books we were reading, and Scott continued to make an effort to get out more and sightsee. He was able to send me pictures from his phone, so everything felt very immediate.

We never Skyped or engaged in any type of video chat. I'm not sure why. I suppose we both preferred to keep some sort of emotional distance between us, because he was still my neighbor from across the street, former husband to my former best friend. Written correspondence felt more appropriate.

Whenever Bev came home from her shift at the hospital and found me typing away at my laptop, she left me alone and didn't interrupt. But the week before Scott was due to arrive home, she asked me a question while we were preparing dinner.

"So what's going on between you two?"

"Nothing," I replied as I tossed the salad.

She moved around the table to set out our plates and cutlery. "But you talk to each other every night."

"We're just friends," I said, "and we don't actually *talk*. We just type and write."

"Still…" She went to the cupboard to fetch two water glasses. "It's fairly intimate, don't you think? The things you talk about?"

I gave her a sidelong glance. "Like I told you, we're just friends. We've both been through hell and it's nice to have someone to talk to who understands. Besides, he's really far away. I think he's just homesick."

Bev nodded. "Maybe. But he's incredibly good looking, right? Surely you must find him attractive."

I laughed and turned around to face her with the wooden salad bowl in my hands. "What are you trying to do here, sis? I'm not even divorced yet, and he's the husband of the woman who stole mine. That would be weird."

I moved forward to set the bowl on the table while Bev served up our chicken breasts with rice.

"I don't think it would be weird at all," she replied. "You know, the same thing happened to Shania Twain. Her husband ran off with his assistant who was also her best friend. Then Shania—who was totally heartbroken—ended up marrying the friend's husband, who was a wonderful man, probably the one she was meant to be with all along."

I shook my head in disbelief. "I am *not* Shania Twain."

"No, but you're a nice person and from what I gather, so is Scott. You might want to think about it."

We both sat down to eat, and I grinned at her. "You're a rascal, do you know that?"

"Maybe." She chuckled. "I just want you to be happy. That's all."

I reached for the salad tongs and filled half of my plate. "Well, I'm not recovered yet from what Wes and Angie did to me, and neither is Scott. I don't want to rush into a rebound situation or date Scott just to get back at them. That's probably what it would look like."

"But don't *not* date him because you're worried about appearances," Bev argued. "If you care for him and he makes you happy…"

I held up a hand. "Stop right there. Scott and I have been pen pals and nothing more. He's my neighbor. I don't want to start imagining there's something happening when there isn't."

"Whatever you say," Bev replied, but I could see that she was skeptical and thought I was in denial.

I decided to let it drop, because my life was complicated enough as it was. I didn't want to start anything that might involve heartbreak down the road. I'd already endured ten times my share of heartbreak this year, and it was only March.

The night before Scott flew home, I offered to pick him up at the airport, but his flight was coming in at midnight and he insisted he take a cab.

Secretly, I was relieved, because I wasn't sure how to behave when we saw each other. If I met him at the baggage carousel, would we hug?

Despite all our personal emails over the past few weeks, he was still just my neighbor. I thought it would be best to maintain a proper reserve, because I didn't want things to get awkward.

He did send me a text shortly after midnight. I was still awake, lying in bed reading a novel when my phone buzzed.

His text said: *Flight just landed. It's nice to be home.*

I immediately sent a reply: *Welcome back to Canada! I'll pop by tomorrow after work and say hi.*

He responded right away: *Great. See you tomorrow.*

I set my phone down on the bedside table and knew in that moment that it was going to be awkward.

It was just past 5:00 p.m. when I rang Scott's doorbell. Butterflies invaded my belly, mostly because I wasn't sure what to expect. The last time we had seen each other in person, we were both in shock over our spouses' affair, and since then, our only communication had been through email. But now he was back, and he was my neighbor again.

The door opened and he smiled warmly at me, in a way he'd never smiled at me before, not when he was with Angie and I was with Wes.

"Hi," he said. "Come in."

I stepped through the open door, and he closed it behind me. Then he looked at me expectantly.

"Welcome back!" I said, giving him a friendly hug.

I felt myself blush as I backed away.

"How's the house?" I asked. "Everything still in the right place? It must seem weird, after being away for so long. I wish I had thought to put some food in your fridge."

I glanced toward the kitchen but remained in the foyer with my coat on.

Scott waved a hand casually. "Don't be silly. You've

already gone above and beyond, changing lightbulbs and whatnot."

We nodded our heads and I smiled clumsily.

Oh, God. This was painful.

"Thanks for all that," he said, referring to my weekly walk-through.

"It wasn't a problem at all. I was happy to do it."

There was a long pause, and I didn't know what to say. I shrugged a shoulder.

"Any more overseas trips planned?" I asked.

What in the world was I saying? He had told me in his last email that he wasn't going anywhere for a while. Probably not even until next year. What a ninny I was.

"Nah, I'll be sticking around," he replied. Then he turned and picked up a gift bag that was sitting on the black leather bench by the door. "These are for you. Bavarian chocolates. I got them in Berchtesgaden."

I reached out to take the bag. "My gosh. Thank you so much." I dug through the tissue paper and withdrew the slender box. "These look amazing. I can't wait to try them."

I slid the box of chocolates back into the gift bag and met Scott's gaze.

Another awkward silence ensued.

"Well, I should get going," I said, gesturing toward my house. "I haven't even been home yet. I came straight here from work."

He watched me with what I could only describe as disappointment, and I wanted to sink through the floor.

What was wrong with me? Had Wes's betrayal stolen all my social skills? My ability to relate to people? I'd never felt so awkward in all my life.

I started backing out the door and Scott said, "Okay, I'll see you later."

He seemed genuinely baffled.

"Bye," I replied as I walked out and descended the stairs.

He shut the door behind me and I crossed the street, shaking my head at myself. "Claire, you are an idiot."

When I entered my house, Bev was just pulling on her coat to go to work for the night shift. "Did you see him?" she asked.

"Yes," I replied, "and it was worse than junior high. I acted like a total nerd. I had no idea what to say."

Her eyebrows lifted. "Oh no! I thought he might pull you into his arms and you guys would end up making out on his sofa."

"Hah!" I began to remove my coat. "Far from it. Not that I would *want* that to happen, but it's so completely opposite from what *did* happen." I squeezed my eyes shut and pressed the heel of my hand to my forehead. "Now it's just going to be *so* awkward between us!"

Just then, the phone rang and I moved to answer it. When I checked the call display, I recognized the number. "Oh, God, it's him."

Bev stared at me while the phone continued to ring. "Well, don't just stand there. Answer it."

I picked it up. "Hi."

This time, there was an intimacy in my tone, as if we both knew why he was calling.

I heard Scott chuckle through the phone. "That was awkward," he said.

I began to laugh—a nervous reaction. "Yes, it was. I'm sorry. I just…I didn't know what to say. This is so weird."

"It is weird," he replied. "And I didn't know what to say either. I've never been in a situation like this before. I'm not sure how we're supposed to act with each other, but I want to be friends, Claire. I don't want you to feel uncomfortable."

"I won't," I said, "now that you've called. I'm glad you did."

"Good."

I felt Bev's eyes on me. She was standing in the kitchen doorway, watching with curiosity, so I turned away and moved toward the back door so I wouldn't feel her presence.

"So listen," Scott said, "why don't we just continue to be neighbors and friends, but I wouldn't say no if you wanted to go to the movies or just play cards or something. I might call and ask one of these days, because it's feeling pretty lonely over here. I could use a friend."

"Okay. Me, too."

"And I couldn't help noticing that the trim around your front window is peeling a bit. I'd be happy to take care of that for you, anytime."

I chuckled again. "You're offering to do yardwork for me?"

"It's not yardwork, it's painting," he replied, good-naturedly. "And I owe you, for looking after my house over the past few months."

I smiled. "Okay, that would be very nice of you. I think we have some of that paint in the basement. I'll have to check."

"If not, I have plenty here," he replied. "It's just standard white exterior."

Neither of us said anything for a few seconds, and I turned

around to check if Bev was still watching me. She wasn't in the kitchen, but I knew she hadn't left for work yet.

"I should let you go," Scott said. "It was nice to see you today, Claire. I mean that."

"It was nice to see you, too. I'll talk to you later."

"Okay, bye."

We hung up and I moved to the living room where Bev was sitting on the sofa with her coat on, her purse on her lap. "So? What did he say?"

I let out a breath and flopped onto the chair. "Well...I don't think it's going to be awkward anymore. He was totally cool about it, actually. He made me feel less like an idiot."

Bev smiled and rose from the sofa. "What did I tell you? Nice guy. Don't screw it up."

I wagged a finger at her. "And don't put pressure on me." I took note of the fact that she hadn't zipped up her coat because she couldn't close it around her belly.

"You need to buy a parka you can zip up," I said. "Have you checked the maternity stores? Stuff is probably on sale now."

She shook her head. "No, it's almost spring. I don't want to spend money on a new winter coat that I'll only use for a month."

"Always so practical," I replied, walking her to the door.

"You should call Scott tonight and invite him over while I'm gone," Bev suggested as she slung her purse strap over her shoulder.

I shook my head. "No, I don't want to set up those kinds of expectations—that we're becoming involved, because I'm not ready for anything like that. I don't know when I will be. I'm still traumatized."

She inclined her head. "You've been traumatized all your life. But as long as you're not still waiting for Wes to realize his mistake and come back to you."

I looked down at the floor. "Of course I'm not. And even if he crawled back on his hands and knees and begged for my forgiveness, I wouldn't take him back. There's too much water under the bridge now."

"Good," Bev said. "Now I have to go. See you later."

I remained in the doorway as she walked out, got into her car and drove off. Then I found myself looking across the street at Scott's house, where it was nice to see lights on in the kitchen, and not just the one lamp in the living room window that was operated by a timer. I was glad he was home.

I stayed up late that night reading the rest of the novel, and it felt odd that Scott and I didn't exchange emails.

More than once, I considered getting up and sending him a message, but I resisted the urge.

He was probably doing the same.

The following day I went to work, and came home to discover a fresh coat of paint on the trim around my front window.

"He doesn't waste time," I said to myself.

I walked in the front door to find Bev cooking spaghetti at the stove. "Hi," she said.

I removed my coat, hung it up in the closet and entered the kitchen. "Were you here when he did that?" I pointed toward the living room window.

She stirred the pasta in the pot. "Yes, but I was sound asleep in my room. Leo didn't even bark. You should call him and say thank you, and invite him over to have dinner with us, because I'm making this huge pot of spaghetti. There's plenty to go around."

I grinned at her as I moved to pick up the phone. "You don't give up, do you?"

"Never."

I dialed Scott's number, and he picked up right away.

"So let me get this straight," Scott said, leaning back in his chair at the kitchen table and sipping his wine while he scratched behind Leo's ears. "The guy doesn't even know he's going to be a dad?"

Bev shook her head. "No. I want to do this on my own."

"But surely he has a right to know," Scott said. "And you need to think long term. What happens when your child grows up and wants to know who his or her father is, and might want to meet him? You can't put all that on the child, to be the one who shows up at this guy's door and breaks the news to him. No kid should have to shoulder that."

Bev rested her elbow on the table and cupped her forehead in her hand. "I honestly didn't think about that, but you're right. I wouldn't want to do that to my child."

Scott shared a glance with me from across the table, and I gave him a look of gratitude. He knew how I felt about the issue—that Bev should tell the guy. I'd been trying to convince her of that for months.

"You're both right," she said. "I know it in my head, but my emotions say otherwise. I just don't want to see him again. I don't want to invite him into the rest of my life—for custody battles over parental rights, and chasing down child support payments. I don't want any of that. And what if he's a total jerk? I just want to do this on my own."

"What if he's *not* a jerk?" I asked. "What if he's the great love of your life and you're not giving him a chance?"

Bev let out a breath, picked up her plate and carried it to the counter. "I don't need a husband to have a baby, Claire, and neither do you."

My head drew back in surprise, because she'd never said anything like that to me before, and here she was, saying it in front of Scott.

She immediately turned to face me. "I'm sorry. I didn't mean it like that. It's just that...this is the twenty-first century and we are strong, independent women. Both of us. We have each other and I believe we can do this. I just want us both to feel empowered and not at the mercy of having to wait for the right man to come along."

Despite how awkward it had been with Scott the day before, I felt surprisingly comfortable with this whole conversation, because he already knew about all my setbacks and insecurities. I had held nothing back from him during our email correspondence, where it was so much easier to be revealing.

"She has a point," Scott said. "You can do whatever you want, Claire. There's nothing holding you back from having a child if you want one. The doctor said you were a good candidate for IVF. Wes isn't here to discourage you or say no to spending the money. Whatever you choose to do is none of his business anymore. You should think about it."

I looked up at Bev, who smiled at me. "There you go," she said. "You have something to think about."

I decided in that moment that I would indeed give it serious consideration. Though it wasn't exactly the traditional dream I'd always had of a house with a white picket fence, a husband, and four or five children, it could be the makings of a new kind of dream with a different sort of family altogether.

Bev was right. This was the twenty-first century. and I was no longer the twelve-year-old girl who had just lost her father. Maybe I needed to let go of my old ideals and be more independent as a woman—because what if I never married again? I had no control over whether or not the perfect man might come along in the future, or *any* man for that matter, and I was about to enter into a divorce that might take years to finalize. Maybe I had to consider the possibility that if I wanted a child, I couldn't afford to wait around for everything to be perfect.

CHAPTER

Twenty-three

Spring arrived before we knew it, and Bev's belly continued to grow. By late May, when pink apple blossoms began to flower in the apple tree in our backyard, we used that for inspiration to decorate the spare bedroom as a nursery, in anticipation of Bev's July 25 due date.

Meanwhile, Scott and I were maintaining a close friendship. There had been no more awkward moments between us, probably because neither of us felt ready to begin a relationship that would, undoubtedly, be complicated. We were both still emotionally scarred from our separations and preferred to keep things platonic.

I felt blessed to have him as a friend, because he was wonderful about lifting my spirits when I felt low. I did the same for him in return.

He was also incredibly handy around the house and was happy to pop by whenever Bev and I needed help with something—like the toilet that wouldn't stop running or a problem with the car. He always had the right tools.

In return, Bev and I invited him over for dinner at least once a week, sometimes two or three times. And when Bev worked a night shift, Scott and I occasionally went out for dinner and a movie, or took Leo for long walks in the park. Scott even started coming to my book club meetings with some of the ladies who worked at my school. He was the only man present, and we all enjoyed his perspective on the books we selected.

He was a good friend during that time, and I was grateful that he lived across the street—especially on one night in particular, when he was keeping me company while Bev was at work, and my world was about to turn upside down all over again.

"Stand up," Scott said, rising from the sofa and offering his hand. "It's really easy. Let me show you."

We had been watching *Grease* on television, and when the dance competition began with Vince Fontaine strutting around the Rydell High School gymnasium, I casually mentioned that I'd always wanted to learn how to jive.

"Come on," he said, offering his hand again.

I looked up at him and smiled. "Are you serious? You know how to jive?"

"Yes, and it's a lot of fun. It's like a happy pill. You can't do the jive without smiling."

"All right." I stood up, and Scott pushed the coffee table up against the sofa so we had more room, then he turned down the volume on the TV.

"It starts with a basic step." He faced me and took hold of my right hand, while sliding his other hand around the small of my back. "Watch my feet. It's like this."

Leo, who was lying quietly in the foyer, watched with

interest as Scott showed me how to rock back onto my right foot, then rock forward, and step from side to side, then repeat the same thing over and over.

"This doesn't seem too hard," I replied, catching on quickly.

"You're a natural." Scott grinned at me as we continued the basic step.

"Now I'm going to spin you around, and you just keep doing this same basic step with your feet, and rocking back as you come around." He lifted my hand up over my head and guided me under for the turn, and my feet continued with the basic step while he counted out the beats.

"That was great," he said. "Let's try it again. Then we'll put on some music and do it for real."

We practiced a few more times, then I went to get my laptop. I set it up on the coffee table and searched YouTube for some music.

"What's a good song?" I asked.

Scott thought about it for a moment. "Try *Crazy Little Thing Called Love* by Queen."

I cued up the song, and soon Scott was leading me through the jive in my living room, and I couldn't believe I was doing it.

"You're right," I said with laughter. "I can't stop smiling!"

"Me neither. You're great at this."

We danced the whole song, then I said, "Can you teach me another move?"

"Sure." He thought for a moment. "I'm not sure what this one is called. It's something like a change of hands behind the back, where I turn, and you stay where you are."

He took me through the move, and soon we were able

to combine it with the step he had showed me before. I cued up the music, and we danced around my living room.

I was laughing when I heard a key in the door. Assuming it was Bev, we just kept dancing. But then Leo started to growl.

It was Scott who stopped us, mid-spin.

I saw his expression change from light to dark in an instant, and then I whirled around.

My stomach dropped, because there—standing in my foyer, staring at each of us in turn—was Wes.

CHAPTER

Twenty-four

"Hey," Wes said, fixing his eyes on mine and patting Leo on the head.

I stood motionless, stunned and speechless, and realized I was still holding Scott's hand. It was ridiculous of me, but I felt a sudden surge of guilt, as if I had been caught cheating.

As soon as I recognized the absurdity of such a reaction, I quickly shook my head. I had nothing to feel guilty about. *Nothing.*

"What are you doing here?" I asked inhospitably.

"I just got off a plane," Wes replied, "and I took a cab straight here. I was hoping to talk to you."

"You could have picked up the phone."

"I wanted to talk to you in person."

I felt my breaths coming faster and faster, like a hot flame of anxiety. "About what?"

While I struggled to remain aloof on the outside, my mind was screaming with rage and a gazillion questions and accusations. All I wanted to do was march forward, grab Wes by the shirt, and shake him senseless, or at least until his teeth rattled. I wanted to pepper him with questions.

What is wrong with you? How could you have done this to us? And why are you here? But I resisted the urge.

Meanwhile, I sensed Scott's wrath simmering in the air beside me—for this was the man who had stolen his wife away. But Scott didn't speak a word. He merely stood there, exerting impressive self-control while he waited for me to take the lead, since it was my home and this was my husband.

Wes glanced briefly at Scott, then back at me. "Can we talk privately?"

It was strange, how many times I'd imagined my husband walking through my door just like this and announcing that he wanted to come home. A part of me wanted him to do exactly that—so that I could have the pleasure of telling him to take a flying leap off a ten-story building. But I wasn't sure if that's why he had come. I had no idea why he was here, and I couldn't deny...I was curious.

Only then did I realize that *Crazy Little Thing Called Love* was still blasting from my laptop. I bent to shut off the music, then took a deep breath and turned to Scott.

"Would you mind giving us a moment? I can call you later."

"Sure," he replied. He moved to the door and said nothing to Wes as he shouldered past him.

I heard the sound of the front door open and close, footsteps down the stairs, and Leo whimpered at his exit. Then suddenly I was alone in the silence of my living room with my soon-to-be ex-husband.

I didn't invite Wes to come in and take a seat because I saw no reason to be polite. He hadn't awarded me any such courtesies when he blindsided me with his sudden departure.

So I simply stood there while he looked around at the walls in the foyer. His gaze traveled up the length of the staircase. Then he regarded me directly.

"The house looks good," he said. "How have you been, Claire?"

My stomach burned with fury, and I scoffed. "Seriously, Wes? You came here to make small talk?"

He bowed his head and shook it. "No. I'm here because I realize I owe you an explanation, and I have something I need to say."

Though I couldn't stop my insides from churning sickeningly, I somehow managed to gesture with my hand for him to enter.

He took a seat on the sofa and glanced briefly at the television, where John Travolta was drag-racing against the leader of the Scorpions. The volume was muted, and the only sound in the room was the clock ticking on the mantel.

I decided to sit in the chair next to the TV, because I wanted to avoid physical proximity with Wes.

"You looked like you were having a good time just now," he said, leaning forward with his elbows on his knees.

"We were doing the jive," I explained.

"I didn't know you knew how."

"I didn't. Scott was teaching me."

Wes stared at me for a moment. "Are you seeing him, Claire?"

I frowned, mostly because it irked me that Wes assumed he had the right to ask me such a question.

"No, we're just friends. We've both been going through a rough time lately. Surely you can understand why. Tonight he told me that jive-dancing was like taking a happy pill. He was right."

I paused a moment, and realized this was not the message I wanted to convey to the husband who had jilted me and broken my trust. "Not that I need a happy pill, Wes. I've been very content with my life these past few months."

He considered that for a moment. "I saw a picture of the two of you sitting with a bunch of other people on a sofa somewhere, and he had his arm around you."

I frowned again. "Where did you see that?"

"On Bev's Facebook page."

I had to think about where that picture had been taken, and then I remembered. "That was a party down the street. The Bakers."

Wes nodded, appearing grateful for the information, while I took into consideration the fact that Bev had posted that picture over a month ago. Had Wes been stalking her page all this time, hunting for news about me, or thinking about what Scott and I were going through? What we were to each other?

Was he jealous?

Even if he was, did it matter?

I laughed bitterly and shook my head in disbelief. "I don't know why I am explaining anything to you. It's none of your business whether or not I'm seeing other people."

"Are there others?"

I shot him a look. "I just said it's none of your business."

Wes backed off slightly and bowed his head again. "I'm sorry, you're right. It's just that…when I saw that picture, I didn't like it. I haven't been able to stop thinking about it. And I've been… I've been doing a lot of soul-searching lately."

"Soul-searching?" I wanted to laugh. "I didn't realize you had a soul."

Wes glanced away. "I suppose I had that coming." He paused, then he met my eyes again. "I think I might have had some sort of mental crisis last fall, and I went a little crazy."

All I could do was sit and listen, still dumbfounded by the fact that he was here—evidently about to express some regret about what he had done to our marriage.

I told myself I didn't care if he felt regret. But I *did* care, because I *wanted* him to feel it. I wanted him to suffer with it. I wanted to grab hold of his head and grind his regret into the pavement in the driveway.

"Does Angie know you're here?" I asked.

Wes shrugged a shoulder. "I'm not sure. We had a big fight and I told her we needed to take a break. I packed a bag and walked out, so she's probably assuming this is where I came. She was pretty mad."

I swallowed over the knot of animosity that rose up from the pit of my belly. Knowing Wes, he probably wasn't answering Angie's calls either. *What goes around comes around.*

"What did you fight about?"

He shook his head bitterly, and I could feel him wanting to open up to me, to pour out all his exasperations and draw out my sympathy.

"What *didn't* we fight about?" he asked. "She's not like you, Claire. She's very...*intense.* At first, that's what I found attractive about her. And she seemed to have so much wisdom about what you and I were going through, and I admired that. I appreciated how she understood my frustrations and was so supportive. Then it just... I don't know. Somehow, it got out of hand, and before I knew it, we were cheating."

He stopped talking and wouldn't look at me.

I felt sick to my stomach. I honestly didn't want to hear this.

"Is that supposed to be some sort of apology?" I asked. "Otherwise, I don't know why you're telling me this. I used to think I wanted to know all the gruesome details about what happened between the two of you, but now..." I sat up straighter. "It's not really something I want to hear."

He finally looked up. "I just need to explain myself, Claire. Please. I need to apologize to you, because this has been tearing me up inside."

"I'm very sorry to hear that," I replied flatly. "But I don't care what you need, Wes, because you certainly didn't care about *my* feelings when you walked out on me in January without any explanation. Then, sending those separation papers so quickly..."

He shook his head. "I know. I'm so sorry. It was Angie who convinced me to cut off all communication with you and move things forward fast—to put it behind all of us. She said a clean break would be best, that it would easier on you and Scott."

I frowned at him. "Are you her little minion? You don't have a mind of your own?"

He wrung his hands together. "Like I said, I went a little crazy."

"Yes, you did, and that's something you're going to have to live with."

Neither of us spoke for a long time. We just sat there in a thick cloud of broody silence.

Then Wes inhaled deeply. "I know I can never make up for what I did, but I have something to tell you, and I wish I had known this before. If I had known it, it might have made a difference. It might have eased some of the strain on us and prevented any of this from happening."

I hated that I was so curious. "What is it?"

He sat back. "A couple of weeks ago, I found out that my father set up a trust fund for me, but he never told me. Apparently he wanted me to make every effort to make my own way in the world, but if that didn't pan out by the time I was thirty-five, he wanted me to have something. Who knew he actually had a generous bone in his body? Certainly not me."

I sat forward slightly. "How big is the trust fund?"

Scott stared at me for a few seconds. "Before I tell you that, I want you to know that I want to try to work things out between us, Claire. You're my wife, and I shouldn't have done what I did. I'm here because I want to ask if you'd be willing to give me another chance."

I sat there in shock and dismay. I had no idea how to respond.

"Does Angie know about the trust fund?" I asked.

He shook his head. "No. Things were already pretty rocky when I found out about it, and it just didn't seem right that she should benefit from it, when you're the woman I married. The one I wanted to spend the rest of my life with."

While I stared at him in astonishment, he cleared his throat and continued. "Please, Claire. I want to come home to you and try to put our relationship back together, and have a baby. We can do IVF or whatever you want, and I swear I'll never complain about it or resist it again. And I'll never betray you or cheat on you, or hurt you. I'm so sorry about what I did." He sat forward, his eyes penetrating. "You *know* me, Claire—better than anyone. That person I was in January... That wasn't the real me. I was under some kind of spell or something. Looking back on it, I can't believe I could have been that stupid, to have walked out on what we had, thinking I'd be happier with her. I wasn't, and it didn't take me long to realize that I'd made a stupid, stupid mistake." He shook his head at himself and looked down at his shoes. "But then...it just seemed so irreversible. So unforgiveable."

I blinked a few times, and struggled to process what he was saying. "So you want to leave her and come home to me...?"

His eyes lifted. "Yes, please. Just give me one more chance. I swear I'll spend the rest of my life doing everything I can to make up it up to you. I just want your forgiveness, and I want the happy life we used to have. Don't you want that, too?"

I let out a breath, and my heart began to pound like a drum.

"Wes, you can't just walk in here and expect me to forgive everything in a heartbeat, and to throw my arms around you and say 'No problem!' What you did *killed* the love I felt for you. You knew my history. You knew how hard it was for me let myself trust you, to believe that you would never break my heart. You promised you would never hurt me, but you did, without the slightest hesitation. You made me *hate* you. How could I ever trust you again after that?"

"Please don't say that," he said. "Your feelings can't be dead. We were part of each other's lives for a long time and I'm certain we're meant to be together. I know we are. We were so good together. You're the most amazing woman I've ever known, and I was an idiot to think it would be better with Angie. She's not as good a person as you are. She can be so emotional sometimes, and clingy."

I looked away, toward the fireplace, because I probably knew more about Angie than he did. I knew her family history, and there was a part of me that understood and sympathized with her fear of abandonment when it came to the men in her life.

Yet, I couldn't allow that to cloud my judgment, because I, too, had suffered the loss of my father, and I had a fear of abandonment. But I didn't go around stealing other women's husbands and cheating on my own. I understood right from wrong.

The next thing I knew, Wes was crossing the room and kneeling at my feet. He took hold of my hands.

"Please, Claire. Let me come home. I'll have the money in a few months and we can put all this behind us and start IVF right away."

I spoke harshly. "What about Angie?"

He shook his head, as if it were a moot point. "It doesn't matter. She'll probably stay in Toronto because she prefers it there. But I don't. This is my home. My home is here. With you."

I slowly slid my hands out of his grasp. "I don't know, Wes. You're making me feel like the money is the thing that will fix what was wrong, and that it's the money that made you come to your senses, but money can't fix the fact that I don't think I can trust you again. And I don't know if I could ever love you like I did, not with my whole heart."

He sat back on his heels, and a muscle twitched at his jaw. "Is it because of Scott? Are you in love with him?"

I frowned. "No! This has nothing to do with Scott. The problem is between you and me."

"Then give me a chance to fix it," he pleaded. "I swear I can earn back your trust, no matter how long it takes. I promise I'll be a better husband. Just let me come home."

Here he was, offering me everything I had wanted in those early days of our separation—my old life back. I could be a married woman again with a lovely house, a devoted husband, and possibly a baby on the way.

But what about the love? The broken trust?

My heart was still racing with anger and indignation, that he felt he could just waltz back into my life and snap his fingers and have me back. It shouldn't be that easy for him. He didn't deserve it.

I firmly shook my head. "You should go. I can't do this right now."

"Why?"

I frowned at him. "I can't believe you would even ask me that! Surely you understand that I need time to think about this and figure out what I want. And don't get all hopeful, thinking it's just a matter of time before I cave, because I'm still *really* mad at you. Right now, all I want to do is kick you out the front door and tell you to go back to Angie in Toronto, because you made your bed there. Go lie in it."

He rose slowly to his feet and looked down at me, where I was still seated in the chair.

"I understand," he said. "This is a lot for you to consider, and I certainly don't deserve your forgiveness. But I'm not going to give up, Claire. No matter how long it takes, I'm going to keep fighting for you. And I'm going to stay right here, so we can keep talking about this."

"Stay *where*?" I asked, feeling a rush of panic. "You can't just move back in here. I realize you're still paying half the mortgage, but Bev lives with me now."

"N-no…" he stammered. "I know that. It's fine. I'll stay with my parents."

I'd had no contact with Wes's parents since he left me in January, and I had no idea how they felt about all this. We had never shared our infertility issues with them, and I hadn't felt that it was up to me to tell them about our separation. But they had never called the house over the past few months, not even to check on me, so I wondered how much they actually knew.

"What will you tell them?" I asked.

"The truth. They already know everything anyway. I confessed the whole thing a couple of months ago, and that's why my mother told me about the trust fund—because she wanted me to come home to you."

I was surprised to hear this, but it didn't make me feel any better.

"So again, the money is the solution to everything." My tone was sarcastic.

"No, it's not," he replied, "but surely it can help us move forward to have the life we wanted. It'll make it easier for us to have a baby."

I looked away. "I don't know, Wes. You're going to have to give me some time to think about this."

I couldn't believe I was actually thinking about it, when I still wanted to kick him out the door. My pride was demanding it.

Wes nodded and turned to go, but he paused in the foyer. "Are you going to be calling Scott now? Are you going to tell him about this?"

I raised my chin. "Probably. He's my friend."

Wes stared at me for a moment, then he let out a deep breath of resignation and walked out the door.

CHAPTER

Twenty-five

As it happened, I didn't call Scott after Wes left. Even though I knew he would be concerned about me, I just wasn't ready to discuss my situation.

Instead, I did chores around the house, like laundry and dishes and other things, while going over everything in my mind. Besides, I didn't know what to tell Scott, or how he would feel about it. I was confused, and I felt disloyal to him somehow, which made no sense because we were supposed to be just friends.

I wondered if Angie had called him. Maybe they were on the phone with each other right now, patching things up. Maybe she was saying terrible things about Wes and trying to convince Scott to take her back.

Would he?

I wasn't sure that he wouldn't, because he was the most honorable man I knew, and she was his wife. A woman with issues. He might very well forgive her and feel a responsibility to take care of her.

But the idea of her moving back in across the street made me want to punch something.

After about an hour, my laptop chimed. I moved to the

coffee table in the living room, opened it up and saw an email from Scott.

Hey there,
I saw him leave a while ago. Do you want to talk?
S.

I carried my laptop to the kitchen table where I could sit down, and typed a reply.

Thank you for checking in. I'm in a state, actually…driven to scrubbing floors and cleaning out my fridge. He said he had a big fight with Angie and he wants to come home. He also just found out that he has a trust fund he didn't know about, which he can collect in a few months, so he wants to try to have a baby with me now. Money solves everything, right? I want to tell him to go stuff it!
C.

I pounded the key when I hit SEND, because I was still so angry about everything.

A moment later, my laptop chimed and another email came in.

Do you want me to come over?
S.

I had originally thought I didn't want to talk about it with anyone, not even Scott, but I changed my mind in a heartbeat.

Yes, please.

Three minutes later, Scott walked through my front door and Leo greeted him with a wagging tail.

I waved Scott into the kitchen, where I was pouring two glasses of wine. He approached me and I handed him one. We gave each other a knowing look, clinked glasses, and took a few big gulps.

"Have you heard from Angie?" I asked, leaning my hip against the counter.

Scott shook his head. "Not a word. So tell me what happened. What did he say? And what did you say?"

I repeated most of it, while Scott listened with sympathy and disbelief. I explained that I was angry more than anything, and couldn't believe that Wes thought he could just walk in here, unannounced, and pick up where we'd left off.

Scott and I talked for over an hour while I ranted about all the reasons why Wes didn't deserve my forgiveness, and why I didn't need him in my life. We never sat down. Scott stood against the counter while I paced around the kitchen.

By the end of it, I was emotionally drained, but I felt better for having let off all my emotional steam. I exhaled a deep breath and turned to Scott.

"I'm sorry for going on and on. You probably regret coming over here now."

"Not at all. You needed to vent. I get it. I'd be pissed, too."

I gave him a small, grateful, heartfelt smile. "Thank you for coming over."

He continued to gaze at me in the brightness of the

overhead light, and I found myself feeling a little lost.

There I stood in the house I owned with my estranged husband, with another man I trusted completely—a man I found very attractive. There was no point denying that fact, even though I'd been denying it for a long time.

But we had both been through the wringer with our marriages, and I wasn't sure *what* I was feeling. In this moment, I liked Scott much more than I liked Wes. I had more respect for him, and there was no anger or resentment between us, because he had never done anything to hurt me.

Yet, my husband had just come home to beg me for a second chance.

"What are you going to do?" Scott asked, his eyes steady on mine.

Suddenly, without warning, my emotions overflowed like some kind of ocean storm surge. I put a hand over my mouth to stop the tidal wave from crashing onto the shore, but it was difficult to hold it in.

Scott strode forward and pulled me into his arms. He held me close while I squeezed handfuls of his denim shirt in my hands and pressed my cheek to his chest. He stroked my hair at the back of my head and whispered, "It's going to be okay, Claire. Everything's going to be okay."

He kissed the top of my head and rubbed my back, and I didn't want to let go of him. I wanted to stay right there, feeling safe and protected in his arms.

"I wish he had never come back," I said. "I was doing perfectly fine without him."

"I know."

With my cheek still pressed tightly to Scott's chest, I breathed in the clean scent of his shirt and closed my eyes, taking deep breaths in an effort to gather my composure.

"I've been feeling so much anger for so long," I explained, "wanting to get back at him for what he did. I wanted him to suffer forever with regret, but at the same time, I don't want to make decisions based on pride or a desire for revenge. He's my husband, and he made a mistake, but now he's begging for my forgiveness and a second chance. We made a commitment to each other, for better or worse. We spoke vows in church, till death do us part."

While I continued to cling to him, Scott simply nodded. He didn't speak. And though I loved how it felt to be held by him, I needed to look him in the eye.

Slowly, I took a step back and wiped the tears from my cheeks. I stared up at Scott and felt his empathy and compassion.

"You have to do what's right for *you*," he said. "And you don't have to make any decisions right now. Take time to think about it. You'll know what's right when the time comes."

"When do you think that will be?"

Scott smiled gently and laid his hand on my cheek. "I wish I knew."

I reached up to squeeze his hand in mine, and kissed his palm.

Suddenly, my blood was racing through my veins.

"What if Angie had been the one to come back tonight?" I asked him. "Would you have listened to her? Would you be able to forgive her?"

"I don't know that either," Scott replied. "I guess it would depend."

"On what?"

He said nothing for a few seconds. Then he shrugged a shoulder. "I don't know. All sorts of things. But she hasn't come back, at least not yet, so I'm just going to keep doing what I've been doing—keeping on with the starting-over part."

I felt myself beginning to relax.

"I thought I was doing so well with that," I replied. "Now it feels like someone kicked me off the road, into the ditch and I can't get up."

He pulled me into his arms again, forcefully, and hugged me tight. We stood for a long while, embracing.

"I should go, Claire," he said after a time, but I didn't want to hear those words.

"Are you sure?"

"Yes. It's late, and tomorrow's a school day. You should get some sleep. Think about everything."

I nodded, but I felt bereft when he took a step back and let go of me.

He was such a good man and I cared for him deeply. He was handsome, loyal, and wonderful. All I could think about was how I didn't want Angie to do what Wes had done tonight—to come home and beg Scott to take her back, because I knew how honorable he was, how forgiving, and how he was sympathetic to her plight. She was his wife, and he had also spoken vows before God and promised to love her forever.

But I wanted her to stay away, so that nothing would have to change between Scott and me.

What did that mean for my own marriage, and the future I truly desired? I wasn't sure, but it didn't make any of this easy.

CHAPTER

Twenty-six

The following morning brought the first day of June—a brand new month with summer vacation just over the horizon, yet I walked home from school with no better clarity than I'd had the night before.

I was still angry with Wes. Part of me hated him for what he had done to our marriage, but I couldn't let go of a sense of obligation to at least consider a reconciliation, because we were still married, and I didn't take that commitment lightly.

Although *he* certainly had.

As I rounded the corner of my street and started walking a little faster, I noticed an unfamiliar vehicle parked in the driveway. It was a black SUV, but as I drew nearer, I recognized it. It was a Range Rover and it belonged to the Radcliffes.

I paused on the sidewalk, wishing that Wes had given me more time, because I didn't have an answer for him yet, nor did I want to be rushed into anything.

The front door of the vehicle opened, but it was not Wes who got out. It was his mother, Barbara.

A swell of nervous butterflies invaded my belly, for I

hadn't talked to her since Wes left, and I had no idea why she was here or what she wanted.

Taking a deep breath and starting off again, I approached and met her at the foot of my driveway, where I stopped and set down my heavy leather satchel full of test papers I had to mark that night.

"Hi Barbara," I said. "This is a surprise."

She wore a cream-colored linen pant suit. Her red hair was swept into a classic twist at the back. She was always so well put-together—a classy, beautiful woman for her age.

She smiled warmly at me, but there was a hint of melancholy about it. "Hi Claire. It's nice to see you."

She stepped forward to give me a hug, and I felt a twinge of sadness and longing for how things used to be.

"Would you like to come inside?" I asked. "I could make some tea."

"That would be lovely, thank you. And I apologize for popping by unannounced, but I was in the area, so I just thought…"

"It's no problem," I replied, leading her up the walk to the front door. "I'm always happy to see you."

I let us in and set my satchel on the bench in the foyer. There was no sign of Bev or Leo, so I assumed she'd taken him to the park.

"Why don't you come into the kitchen and we'll talk while I put the kettle on."

Barbara peeked into the living room. "This house is still as cozy as ever. It was a very good purchase, Claire."

Surprised at the compliment, I spoke over my shoulder as I led the way to the kitchen. "I always thought so. Please, have a seat. Make yourself comfortable."

Barbara sat down at the table while I moved around the

kitchen to fill the kettle and set out a couple of mugs, milk and sugar.

"Wes told me your sister moved in with you," Barbara said. "That she's expecting a child next month?"

"Yes, that's right. It worked out well, since I was here all alone and had plenty of space."

Barbara nodded politely. "Of course. It makes perfect sense."

Neither of us said anything more while I opened the box of tea and set the teabags into the mugs. I carried them to the table and decided to sit down while I waited for the water to boil.

"You're probably wondering what I'm really doing here," Barbara said, rather sheepishly.

"A little… Yes. I haven't spoken to you in a while. Not since Wes left. I wasn't sure where you stood in all of that. You never called."

She raised her chin and sat up straighter. "No, I didn't, and I'm sorry for that. It just seemed very awkward. I wasn't proud of what he did to you, Claire."

I cupped my empty mug in my hands and watched her intently from across the table. "I see."

"That's why I'm here today. To tell you how sorry I am for everything. And I want you to know that we don't blame you. We always loved you, and I don't know what Wes was thinking when he did what he did. I can't say I've been proud of him over the past few months."

The kettle began to boil, so I stood up and moved to turn off the burner. My hands trembled as I reached for the kettle and picked it up. I wasn't sure why. I suppose it was just the whirlwind of my emotions—so many of them all at once. I still didn't know what Barbara wanted from me. Nor did I know what I wanted for myself. But I knew I had to figure it out, soon.

I turned and carried the kettle to the table where I poured the steaming water into our mugs.

"Thank you," Barbara said, reaching for the little jar of milk and pouring some into her cup.

"Obviously," I said, "you must be aware that Wes came here last night?"

"Oh, yes. I was the one who talked him into coming home and trying to put your marriage back together."

"*You* were?" I wasn't sure how I felt about that. I didn't want Wes to simply be following someone else's instructions. If we were going to make this marriage work, he had to want it for himself.

"Don't get me wrong," she said, as if reading my mind. "I didn't have to talk him into it. He was miserable, but he was convinced you'd never take him back. I simply suggested that he shouldn't make any assumptions until he spoke to you, face to face."

I felt nervous all of a sudden, and cleared my throat because I didn't know what to say.

"Claire…" Barbara reached across the table and squeezed my hand. "He told me about your fertility issues. Why didn't you come to us?"

My eyes lifted and I felt a surge of anger because I had wanted to go to them from the beginning, but Wes wouldn't hear of it.

"I wanted to," I told her. "I begged him to tell you, but I think it was my pushiness that drove him over the edge. He didn't want to ask you for money because he was afraid George would say 'I told you so.'"

Barbara nodded. "Wes is very proud. *Too* proud. And

my husband might very well have said just that, because let's face it, he can be a snob sometimes. But now he's had to face the reality that his son was a disgrace for running off with some random woman who clearly seduced him."

I took pleasure in the fact that Barbara referred to Angie as "some random woman." I was glad they hadn't fallen in love with her and preferred her over me.

"She was our neighbor across the street, and my friend," I explained. "Or so I thought."

"Oh, I know all about it," Barbara replied with disapproval. "She must have been a gold digger."

I raised my mug to my lips and took a sip. "I don't know about that. Wes and I didn't know about the trust fund, and besides, her own husband had plenty of money, so that couldn't have been her motivation. I think she's just a very unhappy person with some personal issues."

Barbara rolled her eyes. "Well...I don't know what she was thinking, breaking up your marriage. Obviously she's not a good person, and I think Wes realizes it now."

I nodded and took another sip of my tea.

"So what is it that you want, Barbara?" I asked. "Are you here to try and convince me to take him back?"

She regarded me steadily. "Yes, that is exactly what I want. I also want you to know that George and I are in support of a reconciliation, and that we want nothing more than to see the two of you get back together, and whatever you need financially, we're here for you. I'm aware that Wes told you about the trust fund, which will cover any fertility treatments you need, or even if you wanted to adopt a child from some other country, we would support that and help you in any way we can. I just want you to know that I still consider you my daughter-in-law, and I want you be a part of our family again. I want everything to go back to the way it was. I only pray it's not too late."

I felt a lump rise in my throat because I was touched by her kind words, but at the same time, I wasn't sure I could reconcile with her son. I was still scarred by what he had done to me, and I was confused about what I wanted for myself and my future.

"Thank you for saying all that," I replied. "But I can't make any promises. What he did really hurt me, Barbara, because I loved him with all my heart and I trusted him. I can't simply forget about it at the drop of a hat."

Barbara looked down at her tea. "I understand, and I don't blame you. I just want there to be no doubt that we would welcome you back with loving, open arms, if you could find it in yourself to forgive our son."

As I sat there watching my mother-in-law from across the table, it was clear to me that she was terribly ashamed of Wes.

I was sympathetic, but I still couldn't make any promises.

"I will think about it, Barbara. I give you my word. But I need some time."

"Of course. Take all the time you need. We'll be here, waiting."

She finished her tea, rose from the table, and I walked her out.

When Bev came home from the park and we prepared supper together, I told her about Barbara's visit.

Though Bev had nothing against Barbara personally, she was unsympathetic toward Barbara's anguish and believed they were trying to put pressure on me—to make me feel guilty for not forgiving Wes.

Bev also suggested that they were dangling money in front of me as a way to convince me not to divorce their son.

"Maybe they're afraid you'll go after his trust fund in the divorce," Bev suggested.

I couldn't discount that as a possibility.

"How much is it anyway?" Bev asked.

"I don't know," I replied as I stirred the chicken soup we had taken out of the freezer. "He never told me."

"You have a right to know," Bev replied. "You're still married to him, and I'm no lawyer, but if you do get a divorce, I'm pretty sure you'd be entitled to half of it. Although the Radcliffe's might fight you on that. I'm sure they have high-powered lawyers."

I sighed. "That's the last thing I want—to go through a vicious, ugly divorce. I don't want his money. I just want out."

Bev turned to me, looking pleased. "Really? Have you decided then?"

I let out a breath and stirred the soup again. "I don't know. That just came out. I haven't made up my mind yet. I need more time to think about it."

Bev didn't push the issue. She said nothing more as she set rolls and the butter dish on the table. When everything was nearly ready, she turned to me again. "Should we call Scott and invite him over? There's enough here for the three of us."

I turned off the burner and shook my head. "I don't think we should. It was a bit strange last night."

"How?"

"Well…" I paused and dipped the soup ladle into the pot. "When he came over after Wes left, I cried and he hugged me, and it kind of felt like there was something happening between us. I'm not sure what to make of it. I mean, we've been very close since Angie and Wes left, and there's been a certain intimacy with Scott that I don't feel with anyone else, but last night, it was really nice to be held in his arms. He's just so… I don't know… I felt so comfortable and safe. And he smelled *so* good."

"Finally," Bev replied with a hint of frustration. "Do you know how long I've been waiting for you to say that?"

"Yes, I know."

"He's a wonderful man, Claire, and I'm one hundred percent certain he feels the same way about you. I can tell by the way he looks at you. He's in love with you, but he doesn't want to say anything because he knows you're gun-shy after what happened, and you're both still married, and he doesn't want to behave dishonorably."

I held up a hand. "Please stop. Things are complicated."

Bev flopped down onto a chair at the table and spoke gently. "I know, but I can see what's happening here, Claire. You've always been a tough nut to crack when it comes to love, because of what happened with Dad, and I could absolutely brain Wes for knowing about that and then doing what he did to you. But don't let that scare you off from love forever. Remember, the worst thing *did* happen to you with Wes. Your worst fear came true, but you survived it and you're okay. Focus on that, and be brave and open when it comes to what might be happening between you and Scott."

I considered that for a moment. "I get it. But he's just as confused and unsure as I am. And who's to say Angie hasn't called him today and done the same thing Wes did last night? Maybe she's already asked him to forgive her and take her back."

"And how would you feel about that?"

I didn't even have to think about it. "Horrible. I'd probably want to scratch her eyes out."

Bev squeezed my shoulder. "Now we're talking."

I served up two bowls of soup and carried them to the table. "Let's just have dinner with the two of us tonight, until I figure all this out."

"Fine," Bev replied, "but I don't want to see you lose out because you were indecisive. Don't let Angie beat you to the real prize."

I sat down to eat. "It's not a race. Whatever is meant to be, will be."

"Oh, please," Bev said. "Don't give me that. You can't

just sit there and wait for destiny to choose your future for you."

I sighed. "That's easy for you to say, but I've been knocked around a bit lately and I don't know which way is up."

"Well, I know which way is up." Bev pointed across the street. "It's that way."

I thanked her for her opinion, and picked up my soup spoon.

Wes texted me a number of times over the next few days, and then he called, just to ask how I was doing. I wasn't rude to him on the phone, but I was clear about the fact that I still wasn't sure how much I could forgive. I asked him to give me more time.

He then changed the subject and told me he was trying to get his old job back. I offered no encouragement, because I had no idea if the school would be willing to hire him back, and I certainly wasn't about to ask. Finding a job was his problem.

Then he mentioned that he was considering going back to school for a law degree now that he had the trust fund.

"It could be a new start for us," he said. "And if we had a baby, we could afford for you to stay home and be a full-time mom, even while I was going to school. If that's what you wanted, of course."

I couldn't help but feel that he was dangling carrots in front of my face, saying all the things he thought I wanted to hear, but I wasn't biting. I didn't want this to be about money or status in any way, shape, or form. Besides, I loved teaching.

That night, Scott sent me an email from across the street:

How are you doing? I've been thinking about you. I'm here if you want to talk about anything.

I replied and told him that I'd been thinking about him as well, but I hadn't made any firm decisions.

Then I couldn't help but ask if he had spoken to Angie, because that was my biggest fear—that she, too, had realized her mistake and wanted her husband back. What woman *wouldn't* want Scott?

He responded to my email with this: *Not a peep from Toronto.*

I was overwhelmingly relieved.

Another three days went by, and I was surprised when Wes left me alone completely. He didn't call or text. At first I thought he was giving me the space I'd asked him for, but when I woke up on the fourth day to discover that he had sent me a long-winded email at three in the morning, I sat down immediately to read it, because I knew something was up.

As soon as I read it, I felt sick.

"**D**id you know?" I asked Scott ten minutes later when he invited me into his house.

It was seven in the morning, and he was wearing his bathrobe. I was still in my pajamas because I hadn't wanted to take the time to get dressed after reading Wes's email.

I still couldn't believe it.

Angie was pregnant.

"I had no idea," Scott replied as he led me into his kitchen where the morning sun was streaming in through the back windows. "But I can't say I'm surprised."

He poured me a cup of coffee.

"Why not?"

"Because it sounds like something Angie would do. She is master manipulator, and her timing is impeccable."

I sat down at the breakfast bar with my coffee and buried my face in my hands. "Do you think it's true?"

Scott sat down on the stool beside me. "I don't know, but you must have known this might happen. I've been expecting it every day since they left. I'm surprised it didn't happen before now."

I lowered my hands. "Me, too, I suppose. But when he came home and it looked like things hadn't worked out between them, I thought that possibility had passed. She told him she only found out two days ago, when she took a test. And guess when she's due."

Scott waited for me to tell him.

"Three days before Christmas."

I let my forehead fall forward onto the breakfast bar and tapped it three times, then turned to Scott again. "How wonderful for them. They'll be home just in time to change the first diaper in a pretty new nursery, and then Santa will come down the chimney and bring all sorts of cute little toys for baby. Imagine the ornaments they'll get for gifts. They'll all say 'Baby's First Christmas.'"

I sighed because I had been dreaming of a special Christmas like that for eons. Each holiday season, I had high hopes that everything would work out for Wes and me. But it never did. Even so, I never gave up hope that maybe *next* year would be the year. *Next* year, I'd have my Christmas miracle. It was always a year away.

I regarded Scott intently. "You don't think she's lying, do you? Just to get him back? Because it sounds almost too perfect."

Scott exhaled heavily. "Honestly, Claire, I don't know. It's quite possible. One thing I do know for sure... Angie doesn't like to lose."

I swiveled around on the breakfast bar stool and held my coffee mug with both hands. I found myself staring blankly at the stone fireplace on the other side of the living room.

"Are you okay?" Scott asked, gently rubbing my shoulder.

I took a deep breath and let it out. "Strangely, yes. This may sound crazy, but a part of me is relieved. Even though my husband is about to walk out on me a second time and go back to Toronto to be with my arch nemesis—who has given him a child when I couldn't—it leaves me exactly where I was a week ago."

I turned to Scott, who was more ruggedly handsome than ever with tousled hair and a shadow of morning stubble on his jaw.

"And a week ago," I continued, "I was feeling pretty good about my single life and all the possibilities for the future." I sipped my coffee and lounged back on the stool while I took a moment to think about everything. "If I'm being perfectly honest, the past few days have been pure hell since Wes came back. I was putting so much pressure on myself to decide what to do, and his mother was putting pressure on me to forgive him, and Bev was pressuring me not to. Now the decision has been taken out of my hands, and all my instincts are telling me that this is exactly what is meant to be."

Scott nodded, and we continued to sip our coffees.

"What about you?" I asked. "Are *you* okay? She's still your wife, and now she's pregnant with another man's child."

He set his cup down on the breakfast bar. "We don't know that for sure yet, but even if it's true…yes, I'm fine. Surprisingly. As far as I'm concerned, they deserve each other."

I found myself chuckling, which was an odd response to all this.

"Did he tell you what they were going to do?" Scott asked. "Is he going to marry her?"

I tried to recall the details in Wes's rambling email—the groveling and the apologies and the regret for putting me through this not once, but twice.

"He said he was going to make every effort to make things work between them and take responsibility for his actions, so I guess that means he intends to marry her. But he has to divorce me first."

Scott nodded. "What about the trust fund? Did he mention that at all?"

"No, and I don't care about that. I'm not going to try and take it from him, but it's a good bargaining chip. The one thing I would like out of this is the house. I don't need alimony because I have a job and I can support myself, but I can't really afford to buy him out."

I finished my coffee and got off my stool to carry the empty cup to the dishwasher.

"Don't worry about doing that," Scott said, rising as well. "I'll take care of it."

"It's no problem." I opened the dishwasher, set my cup on the top rack, and closed the door. "But I need to get going or I'll be late for work. I still have to get dressed." I stopped in the center of kitchen and met his gaze. "This is so weird. I actually feel a huge weight lifted."

Scott rose from the stool and walked me to the door. I put my hand on the knob to leave, but he stopped me.

"Claire, wait…"

I felt a tingle of awareness when he touched my arm. "I'm sorry you had to go through all this."

"I'm sorry we both have," I replied, turning to face him.

Then something came over me. I was struck by the incredible blue of his eyes, sparkling in the morning sunlight streaming in through the back windows, and the way he held himself—with strength and tenderness, simultaneously. Anticipation grew in my heart—a thrilling euphoria that made me step forward, wrap my arms around his waist and press my cheek to his chest.

For a breathtaking moment, we stood there in our pajamas, simply holding each other, lost in a state of wonder, and I felt blissfully free from all the angst of my old life. I felt content, and full of new hope.

I didn't know what the future held, but something felt right about this moment. I knew I couldn't walk away or deny what was growing in my heart—a genuine love for this incredibly kind man.

But still…I had to move slowly. I couldn't rush into anything.

I stepped back and looked up at him. "Thank you for being here. I don't know what I would have done without you these past few months."

"I feel the same way," he replied, stroking my hair away from my face. "And I'm not sorry he's gone, Claire. I'm glad."

I felt a warm glow inside of me, and I smiled.

"I need to get to work," I said, "but I'll call you when I get home. Would you like to come over and have supper with Bev and me tonight?"

"Why don't I cook?" he replied. "You and Bev could come over here and take the night off from cooking."

I could barely suppress my joy. It was bubbling up inside of me with gusto. My cheeks felt hot and I wanted to dance. "That sounds great. I'll see you tonight."

I kissed him on the cheek, then turned and ran down his steps. As I jogged across the street, I hoped none of our neighbors were peering out their windows, or they might presume this was a walk of shame after a night of wild impropriety.

Far from it. There was no shame here. No impropriety. Only happiness and goodness.

I just wish it could have lasted longer than half of one perfect, single day.

CHAPTER

Twenty-nine

It's never a good thing when the director of the school knocks on your classroom door in the middle of the afternoon and tells you there's an urgent phone call you need to take.

Principal Jones took over for me in my classroom, and I hurried to the office with knots of apprehension in my belly. My pulse was throbbing so fast and hard, I was lightheaded when I met the secretary's gaze and saw that she had no color in her face. She merely handed me the phone without a word.

I took a breath and spoke into the mouthpiece. "Hello? This is Claire."

"Hi Claire, it's Barbara." My mother-in-law's voice trembled as she spoke. "I'm very sorry to tell you this, but Wes got off the plane in Toronto this morning and got in a cab to go home to his apartment. There was a terrible accident on the 401. A tractor trailer lost control and slammed into the guardrail. It jack-knifed and collided with a bunch of cars. Wes was in one of them."

I sank onto a chair next to the secretary's desk. "Oh, my God. Is he okay?"

Barbara took a few seconds before she replied. "No, I'm afraid not. He died at the scene." She paused to collect herself, then managed to continue. "They say it was instant. He wouldn't have felt any pain, and he probably didn't see it coming."

I couldn't speak. I couldn't even blink or breathe. "Oh, Barbara…"

"I have to go," she said. "I'll let you know more when I can."

She hung up the phone, and I hung up as well. Then I turned in a daze to the secretary who was quietly weeping.

"I'm so sorry," she whimpered. "You should go home, Claire. Mrs. Jones said it was okay, and you don't have to come in tomorrow."

"Thank you," I replied, as I rose numbly from the chair, then walked down the hall to the staff room to collect my belongings.

CHAPTER

Thirty

I can hardly bear to write about the following week's events. I will say only that I attended Wes's funeral in St. Margaret's Bay where he was buried in the Radcliffe family plot.

It was a dark, overcast day. Angie was there, but we did not speak to each other. I saw no evidence of her pregnancy, but of course there wouldn't be any, because she was only a few weeks along—if she were truly pregnant. I still wasn't convinced.

Scott attended the funeral as well and sat alone at the back of the church. Unlike me, he did speak to Angie. I saw them outside the church immediately following the service. The wind was blowing hard and I tried not to stare. They spoke only briefly. He kissed her on the cheek, then she walked quickly to her rental car and drove off. I wondered what they had said to each other.

Angie did not attend the family gathering at the Radcliffe house after the burial. I'm not sure why. Perhaps she knew how they felt about me and she didn't feel welcome. Or perhaps they simply hadn't extended an invitation to her. I didn't ask.

When it was over, I returned home with Bev for a quiet evening.

Shortly after ten, Scott sent me an email. It said simply: *Rough day. How are you doing?*

I sat down and typed a response: *As good as can be expected. It's all such a shock. How are you? I saw you talking to Angie outside the church. She must be taking it hard.*

I sat and waited for him to reply, which seemed to take forever while my belly turned over with nervous knots.

Finally, my laptop chimed.

Yes, I spoke to her, and then I went to her hotel.

My heart dropped. I sat forward, reading his message as fast as my eyes could focus on the words.

We talked for hours. She was very emotional and she cried the whole time. She apologized for what she and Wes did to us, and I had to convince her that he didn't die because they were being punished for it. Sometimes bad things just happen and there's no explanation. He was just in the wrong place at the wrong time.

But I can understand her guilt, because if she hadn't begged him to come back to her, he would still be alive.

Scott

I felt a stabbing of fear, because if they had talked for hours, surely they must have discussed their relationship.

Perhaps, now that Wes was out of the picture and Angie might be pregnant, she would want her husband back. Of course she would. She would be shaken by this sudden loss and terrified for the future, to be raising a child alone. She would be overcome with grief and loneliness.

I wanted to type the words: Does she want to get back together with you? I resisted, however, because it seemed selfish.

Instead, I wrote: *I can only imagine what she must be going through. That must have been very difficult for you.*

Knowing Scott the way I did, I had to assume that he'd held her in his arms and done his best to comfort her. The image made my insides twist into a tight band, because even though I was devastated by Wes's death, I still had feelings for Scott.

But it certainly wouldn't be appropriate for me to act upon those feelings. Not now—the very night of my husband's funeral…

Scott replied:

It was. She was a mess. She asked me to stay with her at the hotel tonight, but I told her I couldn't. Surprisingly she understood why I didn't want to, and she didn't pressure me. She's flying back to Toronto first thing in the morning.

I exhaled sharply with relief, but I still wasn't convinced she wouldn't want him back eventually, especially if she were pregnant and alone.

I decided to be forthcoming.

I hope she'll be okay. She has some support in Toronto, right? She has friends? Because I have to say it… I don't want to lose you, Scott.

Seconds ticked by like minutes while I sat in my chair, chewing my thumbnail and waiting for his response.

What frightened me was that he was such an honorable man. Angie was still his wife, and I could imagine him feeling an obligation to hold true to his marriage vows. I was terrified that he would put an end to the love that was blossoming between us.

Finally, an email came in.

I don't want to lose you either. Let's not give up on this, okay? I understand that you have to mourn for Wes, but I'll be here, waiting for you patiently. And I won't be reconciling with Angie. She doesn't love me, and I don't love her. Not anymore. We both know it. We talked about that today, at length. So that's not a possibility, okay? I don't want you thinking about that.

S.

My whole body shook with relief, and I bowed my head, taking a moment to let my tears flow as I said a prayer of thanks for the words he had written.

All I wanted to do was get up from my chair and cross the street to be with him right away. But we had buried my husband that afternoon and I was still grief stricken. I didn't want to confuse my need for comfort and solace with what might be possible for us in the future.

I typed my reply:

Thank you, Scott. I'm so happy to hear that. I admit I was worried because you mean so much to me. And if the situation were different, I would be on your doorstep right now, stepping into your arms, but that can't happen. Not today. I'm still in shock about Wes's death and I need to come to terms with it. But please don't give up on me.

C.

He replied immediately:

I won't. Get some sleep. I'll be in touch again, and don't hesitate to call or text if you need anything. I'm here for you.

S.

I went to bed and managed to get only a few hours' sleep, because I kept waking up and thinking about the car accident and what it must have been like for Wes in those terrifying final seconds.

I cried for him and wished I could have done something—*anything*—to keep him from getting on that plane. I couldn't help regretting the fact that we never actually said goodbye, and that he had died believing I hated him.

I didn't hate him. I only hated what he did to us.

The following day, Barbara called me to set up a meeting with their lawyer in Halifax, because evidently, Wes had left a will.

I was surprised to hear this, because he and I had not prepared wills together, though we often talked about the necessity of it and had planned to get around to it eventually.

Barbara did not disclose any of the details over the phone. She merely told me what time to meet her, and gave me the address.

Thirty-one

"**Y**ou must be in shock," Bev said that night when I arrived home from the appointment with the lawyer and collapsed on the living room sofa.

I was dressed all in black, though I had felt out of place when I walked into the lawyer's office and was greeted by a bouncy receptionist wearing a brightly colored floral sundress. *Kokomo* by the Beach Boys had been playing in the waiting room. The only things missing were palm trees and cocktails.

Then Barbara and George arrived, both dressed in somber black as well, so I no longer felt like I was in some sort of peculiar dream.

"He was their only child," I said to Bev, "so it was really hard for them to get through that. And like me, they had no idea he'd written a will."

"I feel so bad for them," Bev replied as she sat down beside me on the sofa. "Was Angie there?"

"No. She wasn't mentioned at all as a beneficiary. He left everything to me, which seems strange, considering she was carrying his child and he was separated from me, but apparently, he wrote the will when we were still together, before he started having the affair."

Bev frowned. "Are you worried she'll come after you for child support or something?"

"That did cross my mind, but Barbara and George told me not to worry about that, because they didn't believe she was pregnant in the first place. But even if she is, they said they would take care of it, and that I shouldn't give it another thought. Barbara also told me to keep the silver baby cup she gave me for Christmas the year before last. She said she wanted me to have it because she knew in her heart that Wes considered me the great love of his life, and that he believed his affair with Angie was a mistake. She told me that she believed he would be happy knowing that I was getting his trust fund, and that he would want me to have a good life."

Bev sat back. "Wow. I'll bet he didn't even want to go back to Toronto when Angie told him she was pregnant. He probably doubted she was telling the truth, and he may have said so to Barbara."

"That's what it sounds like," I replied, "but either way, I believe he was trying to do the right thing by going back to Angie, and Barbara believes that he genuinely regretted what happened between us. She said she was certain that if Angie hadn't called to say she was pregnant, he would never have gotten on that plane. He would still be here, trying to win me back."

"Gosh… What did you say to that?"

"I just nodded my head, and let her believe that we might have worked things out. Maybe we would have. I don't know. But I could see that she really needed to believe that. She wanted to imagine that we would have gotten back together and given her and George lots of beautiful grandbabies."

Bev reached for my hand and squeezed it. "Come on into the kitchen. You must be starving."

I followed her out of the living room.

Later, when we turned on the evening news after dinner, Bev turned to me. "You still haven't told me," she said.

"What's that?"

"How much money he left you."

Suddenly, I felt as if I were falling. My whole body went numb as reality began to sink in, and I experienced a painful twinge of guilt. "He left me the trust fund and the house, which had mortgage insurance, so if either one of us died, the whole thing gets paid off."

Bev sat forward, gazing at me impatiently. "How much is the trust fund?"

I swallowed uneasily and cleared my throat. "Two million dollars."

Bev's mouth opened. "Two million dollars? You're not serious."

"I am."

"And the Radcliffe's are okay with you keeping all of it?"

I nodded. "They said they want me to have it, because that's what Wes would have wanted." I regarded my sister with a frown. "I just hope Angie doesn't come after me, because I'm sure she'd feel differently about that, considering that he was on his way back to Toronto to be with her and not me. And if she truly is carrying his child, Bev, I don't think I would feel comfortable keeping it."

My sister pulled me close for a hug I desperately needed.

CHAPTER

Thirty-two

Weeks passed, and slowly I returned to my regular routine at school, which mostly involved preparations for summer vacation. Scott and I maintained a friendly distance during that time, which seemed the right thing to do. But I always felt his presence across the street and drew comfort when I saw the lights come on in his front window at night.

I didn't hear a single word from Angie, and I wondered if she might have simply disappeared from our lives forever, which was quite possible if there was no baby. At least she was back in Toronto among her friends at work, and I didn't have to worry about bumping into her somewhere unexpected.

When school let out, I focused on Bev, who was due to deliver her baby at the end of July. She was uncomfortable when the weather grew humid and warm and chose to leave her job a few weeks early for maternity leave. After that, she and I often escaped to the beach or a movie theater on hot afternoons, because we had no air conditioning in the house.

Then the trust fund arrived in my bank account—right in the middle of a heat wave—and the first thing I did was install a heat pump, which provided more economical heating in the winter and cool air in the summer. It was a sensible purchase that would save energy and improve my utility bills in the future.

Other than that, I didn't touch the money. I consulted a financial advisor who helped me decide how to invest it wisely.

Bev went into labor on July 30, nearly a week past her due date. I was there at her side, coaching her through the pain and holding her hand.

At 6:11 p.m., she gave birth to a beautiful, dark-haired baby girl she named Louise. I fell in love with my niece immediately, weeping tears of joy the moment I held her in my arms.

Though I was willing to help Bev in every possible way at home during her first weeks of motherhood, our own mother insisted on coming to stay with us as well, since neither of us had any experience with newborns.

Those breezy summer afternoons, with the four of us under one roof—three generations of women, all infatuated with a sweet little soul who had brought overflowing love into our home—were very special.

Leo was gentle and loving around Louise. He had a knack for anticipating when she was about to wake up from a nap, and he would trot over to Bev and nudge her with his nose.

Despite my struggles to become pregnant and have a child of my own, I felt no envy or resentment toward my sister, nor any discontent about my own situation. As far as

I was concerned, my joys could not have been more bountiful, and I counted my blessings every day.

But of course, it could not be smooth sailing forever…

Sixty days after we buried Wes, a courier arrived at my door and delivered a large manila envelope. When I saw that it had come from a law firm in Toronto, I knew exactly what it was, and my heart sank because it reminded me that I was not as free of my old life as I had begun to believe.

My precious new beginnings still carried relics of pain from past betrayals—not only surrounding my husband, but surrounding the woman who had pretended to be my best friend.

Thirty-three

Not wanting to worry my mother or sister, I called Scott and arranged to have dinner with him at his house that night. I wanted to talk to him because he was smart about money and investments and legal matters, but more importantly, he knew Angie better than anyone, and I would have felt lost without his advice.

Before dinner, while lasagna cooked in the oven, we sat down on the leather sofa in his living room, so that he could look over the documents.

When he finished, he sat back and said, "Wow."

"I know," I replied. "I'm still processing everything. But it's pretty clear what she wants."

He nodded. "She's suing you for Wes's entire trust fund."

I stood up and walked to the kitchen to pour the wine that had been left to breathe on the counter for the past twenty minutes. I poured two glasses, returned to the sofa, and handed him one.

"You weren't even sure if she knew about the fund," Scott said as he accepted the glass.

I sat down beside him. "That's right. When Wes came

to see me, he told me that she didn't know anything about it. I can only assume that he revealed it after he agreed to return to Toronto, when she told him she was pregnant."

Scott pointed at the papers on the coffee table. "And this is very clear that she is pregnant, just past the first trimester. She's arguing that despite the will he wrote, he wouldn't have wanted the money to go to you, not when he had a child on the way."

"That could be true," I said. "And to be honest—as much as I dislike Angie—she's about to give birth to his child, and it doesn't feel right that I should be the one to receive the giant nest egg he left behind. He filed that will before he knew about the baby. And though I would love to be a millionaire, I find myself wondering… What would my father do in this situation? How would *he* want me to handle this?"

Scott watched me carefully. "And? What's the answer to that question?"

I sighed. "I don't think I could live with myself if I fought her over this." I regarded Scott intently. "I never felt right about it, you know. Because I'm not even sure I would have taken him back. I probably wouldn't have."

We both sat for a moment or two, listening to the soft jazz playing on his portable speaker, and breathing in the delectable scent of lasagna in the oven.

"So what are you going to do?" Scott asked.

I sipped my wine. "I'm not a hundred percent sure, but I'll definitely talk to a lawyer. Right now, I'm leaning towards handing over the money."

Scott regarded me with astonishment. "Really."

"Yes, but I'm not just going to hand the whole kit and caboodle over to her without making sure it's put to good use. After what she did to me—and us—I'm still angry with her and I don't think she deserves a giant windfall like this. I wish I didn't feel that way, but I do. What can I say? I'm only human, and I feel very little sympathy toward her, even though she lost Wes, too."

I paused and sipped my wine.

"But that's not what matters here," I continued. "It's the child I can't stop thinking about. Wes's child, who is completely innocent in all this. The money should go to him or her. So there's got to be a way to settle with Angie somehow, to get her to agree to accept some sort of annuity to raise the child, while most of it remains in trust for when he or she reaches the age of majority." I set down my wine glass. "I just don't want to hand two million dollars over to Angie without any parameters, then watch her blow it on herself, on trips and shoes. Do you think she would do that?"

Scott sat forward. "I don't know. Maybe she would blow through some of it, but she's not stupid. She'd want to make it last."

I tucked a lock of hair behind my ear. "Sadly, two million dollars doesn't go all that far in this day and age, especially with the cost of living in Toronto, and the cost of education if the child wants to go to university down the road."

Scott watched me while I turned everything over in my mind. "I have a feeling you've made up your mind," he said.

"Yes, I think I have." I took a deep breath.

"So that's what you're going to do? Give her the money?"

I sighed heavily and nodded.

Scott glanced over the papers. "Didn't his mother tell

you that if Angie ever came after you for the money, they would take care of it? They are the grandparents after all."

I considered that while I took another sip of my wine. "Barbara did say that, and she tried to convince me that Wes would have wanted me to have the money, not Angie— probably because she knew how guilty he felt over what happened. But I'm okay now. I'm alive and I'm happy. My house is totally paid off and I have my sister and her newborn baby living with me, and I love them both. Besides, it's not up to Barbara. It's *my* money now and I can do whatever I want with it. Unfortunately, Wes isn't here to speak for himself, but I have to go with my gut. I may not have known him as well as I thought I did, but I'm pretty sure he would have wanted that money to go to his son or daughter. I don't feel right keeping it for myself. That would feel very greedy, and I'm not a greedy person. I just want everyone to be happy. Even Angie, I suppose."

Scott reached for my hand and held it. "You're an amazing person, Claire. I have to say… I've never loved you more."

I felt a spark of something exhilarating, as if my broken heart had just been pieced back together. "I didn't know you loved me *before*."

Scott raised my hand to his lips and kissed the back of it. "Wasn't it obvious?"

We gazed at each other tenderly in the lamplight while Johnny Mathis sang soulfully in the background.

Sliding closer to Scott on the sofa, I rested my head on his shoulder. He wrapped his arm around me and stroked my hair.

"I do love you, Claire," he said softly as he kissed the top of my head, "and I don't ever want to live without you."

I felt an almost ferocious desire for him. "I don't want to live without you either. I've felt this way about you for a long time, but I've been holding back, because everything's been so complicated and painful. But now, Wes is gone and… Still, I don't know if I'm ready."

"I know," Scott said, rubbing his thumb over my shoulder. "We don't have to rush this. We can take it as slowly as you like, but I'm not going anywhere. And you might as well know…"

He paused and looked down at me. I sat back slightly so that I could see his face.

"I have every intention of marrying you," he said. "When you're ready."

My eyebrows lifted, and I couldn't help but smile. "You are presumptuous."

"Not presumptuous," he replied. "*Hopeful.*"

A feeling of electricity sizzled in the air between us as I gazed into the depths of his beautiful eyes. Then he wrapped his big hand around the back of my head and slowly pulled me in for a kiss that left me breathless. His lips were warm and sweet, and he tasted like the full-bodied red wine we had been drinking.

I wanted nothing more than to give myself over to him completely, knowing that my heart would be safe, that he would never hurt or betray me. He was the most honorable man I had ever known, and he was handsome beyond my wildest imaginings. I'd always known it, but now that I loved him openly with my whole heart, he was ten times more attractive than I'd ever dreamed a man could be.

The timer on the oven began to beep, and I slowly drew back. "Is that supper?"

He beheld me with desire and cradled my chin in his

hand. "Do you know that you are the most beautiful woman on the face of the earth?"

I grinned. "No, but I love that you think so."

The beeper went off again and he chuckled softly. "I should go and take that out of the oven before it burns."

"I suppose. Let me help you."

We both stood up and he led me to the kitchen, never letting go of my hand until he had to pull on the oven mitts. He opened the oven door and steam filtered out. The lasagna was covered with golden mozzarella cheese and fragrant fresh oregano that filled my senses. I felt positively intoxicated with happiness.

I closed my eyes and breathed in the heady fragrance, then I went to the table to light the candles and open another bottle of wine.

P art of me felt guilty for retaining the services of a lawyer and handling the matter of Wes's trust fund on my own without ever telling his mother about it. But I didn't want Barbara to try and talk me out of it, which I was quite certain she would do because it had been their money, after all.

During the few times we had spoken about Angie, it had become apparent to me that Barbara felt no affection for the woman who had lured her son away—not only from the sanctity of his marriage, but from his family home in Nova Scotia.

That's why she hadn't invited Angie to the reception after the funeral service and burial. She was as angry with her as I was.

But that was before any of us knew with certainty that Angie was carrying Wes's child. Now it was certain. DNA tests had been performed, and it was time for me to do what I believed to be the right thing.

Two months after I received the papers from her lawyer, just after Thanksgiving, when colorful autumn leaves lay crisp and dry on the ground, blowing in the wind, we settled out of court. I agreed to a full transfer of the principal amount of the investment funds, and Angie agreed to my stipulation that a reasonable annuity would be paid to her each year for the raising of her child. This was to be managed by an independent trustee and dispersed accordingly. As long as the funds were managed sensibly over the coming years, Wes's son or daughter would receive the full balance that remained when he or she reached the age of majority.

I was happy with this arrangement, and Angie seemed happy too, though I never spoke to her directly. It was all handled through lawyers.

When everything was settled and I was no longer in possession of the money, I felt a tremendous weight lifted, but it was mirrored by an uncomfortable ache in my heart, for I had never revealed any of these proceedings to Barbara, nor had I sought her advice. I had simply made up my mind, on my own.

I felt an intense need to speak with her and George and let them know what had transpired. I wasn't sure how they would feel about what I had done (Bev thought I was crazy for giving up the money) but I knew that Barbara was a reasonable woman who had loved her son more than anything in the world.

I had loved him, too. All I wanted was peace for everyone involved.

So I sat down at the kitchen table one evening after Bev and the baby were asleep, and I picked up a pen to write a letter to my mother-in-law, longhand.

Dear Barbara,

I'm sorry for not calling or visiting you since the funeral, but life has thrown a few curveballs my way. The first one was a happy ball to catch, as my sister Bev went into labor at the end of July and delivered a beautiful baby girl named Louise. Mother and daughter are doing well, and Bev has been enjoying her maternity leave. She still lives with me, and I, too, have enjoyed the pleasure of being an auntie. It's a very nice arrangement.

But that is not why I am writing. I'm not sure if you've heard anything from Angie lately, but she contacted me in August to let me know that she was expecting Wes's baby in December. Actually, she had her lawyers contact me because she wanted to challenge the will. She asserted that Wes's true wishes had not been reflected in the will that he had written last summer, before he knew he was going to be a father. She asked that I relinquish the trust fund, so that she would have some support while raising their child alone.

I hope you understand, but I decided that it would be best to give the trust fund to Angie's child. I transferred the full amount a few days ago, and arranged for it to be managed by a trustee over the next twenty-one years, after which time the balance would be transferred to the child.

I feel good about this decision, and I hope you understand.

But there is much more I wish to say, and this is the most important reason for my letter. I'm sure you've noticed that I have enclosed a Christmas gift box with this package, which is tied up with a red and green ribbon. This may surprise you, as it is only October and not yet the holiday season, but I didn't want to wait.

In it you will find the lovely silver baby cup and spoon you gave to me the Christmas before last.

I am returning it to you now so that you may reach out to Angie and offer this to her as a gesture of love. Her due date is December 23rd, and after she delivers her child, she will return to her apartment alone. She has no parents of her own—they passed away many years ago—so it is my hope that you will welcome your grandson or granddaughter into the world with loving arms, and forgive her for the unconventional beginnings of her relationship with Wes. I have come to terms with it, and I believe in my heart that Wes was meant to love Angie and she was meant to love him, for they have created something beautiful together—a new life, something he and I were never able to accomplish during the time we were together.

I don't know why he was taken from us. Only God knows the answer to that question. But we all must continue to march on through life, trusting that it is unfolding the way it is meant to.

Please take this baby cup that was so special to you after you brought Wes into the world. Get on a plane and visit the woman who will give birth to your grandchild. Love her unconditionally and forgive her for everything. I am working toward that myself.

With deepest love and affection,

Claire

CHAPTER

Thirty-five

A month and a half later, December arrived, and all the charming Victorian homes in my neighborhood boasted outdoor lights and festive wreathes on doors. Christmas music played in the shopping malls, and there was a joyful bustle to life that only existed during the holiday season.

Giant snowflakes fell gently from the sky as I walked home from school in my down-filled overcoat, wearing my favorite red woolen scarf and mittens, carrying my leather satchel full of end-of-term tests to mark. As I rounded the corner of my street, I spotted Barbara's SUV parked in my driveway.

Pausing on the sidewalk, I felt a pang of apprehension because I hadn't heard a word from her since I'd sent the silver baby cup and spoon and informed her of my decision to hand Wes's trust fund over to Angie. I still felt guilty about not involving Barbara and George in the decision, and I worried that she might be angry about that.

Starting off again and turning into my driveway, I noted that the vehicle was empty. I could only presume that Bev had invited Barbara inside.

When I entered the house, I found them seated in the living room next to the Christmas tree, with the silver tray and formal tea set arranged on the coffee table. Bev had set out a plate of store-bought cookies, while Louise lay in her playpen in the corner of the room, making baby noises. Leo slept quietly in the foyer.

As always, Barbara was impeccably dressed in an expensive black pant suit and heels, with a heavy gold chain and gold button earrings, her red hair swept into the usual elegant twist.

Bev looked up when she saw me, and I sensed her relief at my arrival. She immediately set down her teacup and greeted me.

"Hey, look who came by. Barbara and I have just been sitting here, chatting about the American election."

I set down my satchel and approached Barbara, who rose from her chair to hug me.

"It's so nice to see you," I said. "Merry Christmas. Let me hang up my coat."

While I unzipped it and moved to the front closet, I was aware of Bev gathering up the tea tray. When I returned to the living room, she was rising from the sofa to carry it to the kitchen. She shrugged as she passed by, as if to say she had no idea what, specifically, Barbara had come about.

I joined my mother-in-law in the living room and we made small talk for a few minutes, catching up on the usual things—in particular how much we both missed Wes and how especially difficult it was to be without him during the holidays.

Bev returned to collect Louise and explained that it was time for her feeding. A moment later, Barbara and I were left alone.

I cleared my throat as we sat in awkward silence. Then I decided to approach the uncomfortable subject of why she was here.

"I assume you got my letter," I said.

"Yes, Claire, I did." Her cheeks were flushed, her expression intense, and I worried that she intended to reprimand me. Instead, she raised a tight fist to her lips and began to cry.

I quickly reached for the box of tissues on the end table beside me and crossed the room to offer it to her. She accepted it, and dabbed at the corners of her eyes.

"I apologize," she said as she made an effort to collect herself.

"No need, Barbara. It's been a difficult time." I returned to the sofa and sat down again.

She took a moment, then she began to explain herself, without ever meeting my gaze. "At first when I read your letter, I was very angry with you, because I despised that woman who took our son away. I hated her with every breath in my body, because if it weren't for her, Wes would still be alive today and he would never have left us or sunk so low as to betray his marriage vows to you." She paused and took a breath. "I didn't want her to benefit from money that came from us, indirectly, and George was just as angry as I was. He was talking about hiring lawyers to try and get it back from her, but of course we knew that would be impossible."

She pulled out another tissue and blew her nose, then eventually continued. "I didn't open the gift box you sent. I knew what was inside it, but I just couldn't face it. I knew that if I looked at it, I would be taken back to that moment when I first held Wes in my arms—he was such a precious little darling—and it would rip my heart to shreds all over again."

She laid her open palm on her chest and spoke passionately. "The pain is so deep, Claire, I cannot even describe it to you."

My stomach muscles clenched as I fought to hold back tears, because no mother should ever have to endure the death of her child.

For a moment, we sat in silence. Barbara's elbow was perched on the armrest of the chair, her chin resting on her knuckles. Then she took another breath and continued.

"So I put the gift box away where I couldn't see it, at the back of my closet, and I tried not to think about it. But then…" She cupped her hands together on her lap. "I woke up one night at four in the morning, dreaming that Wes was in his crib in the nursery, crying for me. I was half asleep and I actually got out of bed and hurried down the hall to his old room. I was sleep walking, I suppose, and when I realized where I was, and that he wasn't with us anymore, my heart began to pound. I was so confused and distraught… It was as if I had traveled back in time and he was a baby again, but when I turned on the light, it wasn't his nursery. It was just my sewing room. But the dream was so real. I was sure I heard him crying for me, and the heartache and longing I felt was so intense, I couldn't go back to sleep. I wanted him back so badly…"

She turned her eyes to the Christmas tree in the corner of the room near the front window. She stared at it for a long time while I said nothing.

She continued. "So I went to my closet and found your Christmas box, took it downstairs so that I wouldn't wake George, and I opened it. When I saw the cup and spoon, I thought about Wes's unborn child, and it was as if a light came on inside me. I couldn't believe how foolish I was being, letting my anger at that woman eclipse the fact that he had left us with a grandchild—a child who would never know his father."

She cried again for a moment, and I stood up to pull a tissue out of the box for myself, for I was quite emotional by this point.

Barbara regarded me steadily. "I know how badly you were hurt by what he did to you, Claire, but when you said in your letter that you were working toward forgiving Angie, I felt ashamed. You are a very special woman—feeling love for your enemy instead of hate, and putting your pride and jealousy aside in order to do what was right. You made me see that I needed to do that, too. And so did George. So we have taken your words to heart, and we're going to Toronto to meet the mother of our grandchild, and we fully intend to open our hearts to her and welcome her into our family."

I bowed my head and wept into the tissue.

"I hope that doesn't make you feel that we are choosing her over you," Barbara said. "You are the last person in the world I would ever want to hurt or betray."

"Of course not," I replied. "She's the mother of your grandchild. It's the right thing, and I would never resent you for that. I'm happy, Barbara. We've all been through a terrible year, but it's time for something good to come from it."

Barbara smiled at me with love. "No one deserves happiness more than you do, Claire. Wes was a lucky man when he married you, and he was a fool to let you go."

We stood up and shed a few more tears as we hugged each other in front of the Christmas tree.

When I said goodbye to her at the door a few minutes later and watched her drive down the street, through fresh falling snow, past all the houses lit up with colorful Christmas lights, I felt an inner peace I had never known before. Not like this. And I hoped that when Barbara and George visited Angie in Toronto, she would accept the love they offered, and that they, too, could find some measure of peace this holiday season.

I turned to go back inside, closed the door behind me, and went to call Scott.

Scott's divorce did not become final until the following summer, but that was just a formality, for we were deeply in love by then and totally committed to each other. Neither he nor I had any illusions about the fact that we fully intended to spend the rest of our lives together.

However, being the honorable man that he was, he waited until the papers arrived to prove that he was a free man before he got down on one knee on the rocks by the century-old lighthouse at Peggy's Cove.

"Claire," he said as the sunset lit up the sky in splashes of pink and blue. "I've never known any woman with such a good heart, so beautiful on the inside as well as the outside. I'm still astonished that we found each other when we had already pledged our hearts to others. But I believe that we were meant to come together the way we did, and discover in each other a soft place to fall. I love you more than anything. I vow to always be by your side, faithfully." He reached into his pocket and withdrew a black velvet box, which he opened in the magnificent changing light of the setting sun. "Will you marry me?"

Tears spilled down my cheeks as I laughed and nodded

my head and said yes, without hesitation. My hand trembled as he slid the ring onto my finger and pulled me into his arms for a passionate kiss while the waves crashed thunderously on the rocks below.

"I was thinking that we could tie the knot this fall," Scott said, as we strode, arm-in-arm, toward the car to drive home. "Somewhere quiet and intimate with a few of our closest friends and family."

I paused outside his car while he insisted on opening the passenger side door for me.

"That sounds like a dream," I replied, before I got in. "I've already had a big splashy wedding, and we both know how that turned out. I don't need the white dress or a fortune spent on flowers and hors d' oeuvres. I just want to be your wife."

I was still smiling when he pulled me into his arms again and kissed me.

It was a perfect white Christmas that year, like something out of an old movie. I was a newlywed again, living with Scott in his house across the street, which we had redecorated over the summer to suit our own tastes.

Meanwhile, I rented my own home at a very fair rate to my sister Bev, which was a wonderfully convenient arrangement. Not only did it allow me to be with Scott, but it also allowed me to continue to be a devoted aunt to little Louise and help Bev out with childcare whenever she needed it. It was good to be close by.

With each passing day, I fell more and more in love with my beautiful niece, and so did Scott. We counted ourselves lucky to have a child in our lives, because neither of us had been blessed with the ability to conceive naturally, but at least we had each other.

Not that we had given up on the hope to have a child of our own one day. We had been seeing Dr. Walker, and we had an appointment in early January to begin IVF treatments. We had decided that we would attempt to fertilize my egg with Scott's sperm, but if it didn't take after six months, we would try a donor.

It was a happy holiday season, full of excitement for what the future might bring. I felt very fortunate and especially happy when Scott said that's what he loved most about me—that I never complained about what we did not have, or the things that stood in the way of our happiness—like the fact that we were both infertile. I only saw the possibilities before us, and focused my attention on the avenues that might circumvent those obstacles.

He was right. I never felt sorry for myself. How could I, when I was married to the most wonderful man in the universe, and I was blessed with a loving family and the miracles of modern medicine?

On Christmas Eve, Scott and I, along with Bev, Louise and Leo, drove to my mother's house for a traditional turkey dinner with all the trimmings, and cheesecake in the shape of a wreath for dessert.

Normally, I was the first to finish my dinner and ask for seconds, but when we sat down at the table, and bowls of mashed potatoes, carrots, and sliced turkey were passed around, I found myself suddenly without an appetite. When the gravy came my way and I took a whiff of it, I felt a sudden urge to gag and had to get up and excuse myself.

I went to the bathroom, shut the door, and splashed some water on my face. Not feeling ready to go back to the dinner table quite yet, I closed the toilet lid and sat down until the queasy feeling passed—because I didn't want to miss out on Christmas Eve dinner. Turkey and stuffing with gravy and mashed potatoes and cranberry sauce was my favorite. Normally I'd be piling everything onto my plate, sparing nothing.

A knock sounded at the door. I stood to open it.

"Are you okay?" Bev asked, looking concerned as she entered the tiny bathroom and shut the door, leaving Leo out in the hall. She placed the back of her hand on my forehead. "You didn't look too good when you got up from the table. You're pale."

"Do I have a fever?" I asked.

She felt my cheeks and shook her head. "No, you feel normal. But poor Mom. She thinks her turkey is undercooked, but I'm sure it's fine."

"It wasn't that." I sat down on the edge of the bathtub. "I don't know what's wrong. I smelled the gravy and I wanted to vomit."

Bev inclined her head. "Do you think you might be pregnant?"

I immediately looked up. "What? No, of course not."

"When was your last period?"

I tried to remember, but couldn't. "I don't know. I stopped keeping track of it ages ago. There didn't seem to be any point."

Bev sat down on the toilet. "Try to think. When was the last time you had one? Have you had one since the wedding?"

Scott and I had been married in mid-October when the leaves were changing, then we flew to Tampa to spend a week on St. Pete's beach. I struggled to remember if I'd had a period since then.

"Yes," I replied, raising my finger. "It was right after we got back from our honeymoon, and I was really glad it didn't start while we were down there."

"Okay," Bev said, as if she were connecting a series of dots, "so that would have been at the end of October. What about since then?"

I wracked my brain, struggling to remember, then I shook my head. "No, I don't think I've had one since then."

Neither of us said anything for a few seconds. Then Bev chuckled. "That's two months, Claire."

We continued to stare at each other in my parents' tiny bathroom, while my heart began to pound a little faster.

No, it couldn't be possible, and I certainly didn't want to get my hopes up again. I'd been down that road too many times—especially at Christmastime—and I couldn't handle any more disappointments. It was so much easier to just forget about it on a day-to-day basis and place my fate in the hands of the medical professionals.

"It's not possible," I said. "Between the two of us, Scott and I are totally hopeless. My tubes are completely blocked and he has weak swimmers. The odds are next to none."

"Stranger things have happened," Bev replied.

No. I didn't want to go there.

"It's probably just a bug," I said, waving my hand through the air, "or something I ate over the last few days. There have been way too many cakes and squares and little meat canapés everywhere we go."

"Maybe," Bev said, "but you should come out and try to eat something, or Mom will think it was something she did that ruined Christmas dinner. And if your period still doesn't start in the next twenty-four hours, we'll get you a test at the pharmacy as soon as it opens."

"Leave it to me to have a pregnancy scare when every drug store in the city is closed for the holiday."

"Yes, that is just your luck," she said with understanding.

We returned to the table and I managed to get through my dinner without gagging. I said nothing to Scott about what Bev had suggested. I'd been through this before, with Wes, and I didn't want to entertain any further high hopes that would likely end in an emotional crash-and-burn situation.

After dinner, we sang *Jingle Bells* by the fire, but Louise began to fuss when the hour grew late, so we packed up and drove home through the gently falling snow.

As we pulled into our cozy little neighborhood of tree-lined streets, I found myself gazing up at the full moon, wondering what I would do if I saw a sleigh with eight tiny reindeer pass in front of it.

I chuckled and shook my head at myself and retreated back to reality.

I wish I could say that I remained sensible and grounded about what was on my mind that night, but when we pulled into the driveway shortly before midnight and said goodnight to Bev, I waited for Scott to go inside the house. He took his time, knocking a few icicles from the eaves, then he disappeared into the house.

I remained outside for a few moments more, alone, where I dropped to my knees in the snow.

Cupping my hands together, I squeezed my eyes shut and began to pray.

Not that I ever had any doubts about marrying Scott, but when he got out of bed on Christmas morning, put on his coat and boots, and pulled the wooden toboggan across the snow-covered street to Bev's house, I was convinced I was the luckiest woman on the planet.

Over a foot of snow had fallen during the night, and the neighborhood looked like a winter wonderland.

I watched Scott from the front window as he piled a giant bag containing Bev's and Louise's Christmas gifts, as well as their stockings, onto the sled. Leo bounced around with excitement at the activity. Scott then hauled it back to our place with Leo running next to him—so that we could open everything together.

While they kicked the snow off their boots and removed their coats, I put on a pot of coffee and filled the creamer with eggnog.

A short while later, Bev carried Louise into the living room and we all sat down to open our presents around the tree.

Scott gave me an exquisite diamond necklace, along with

a DVD copy of *The Sound of Music*, autographed by Christopher Plummer. I nearly fainted.

Then he opened his gift from me—the same DVD copy of *The Sound of Music*.

Mine was not autographed by anyone, but the fact that we had both been thinking the same thing for our first Christmas together was enough to make us feel very sentimental.

Bev and I exchanged gifts as well. She gave me a hardcover novel by an unknown author that she promised I would love, and I gave her a set of six crystal wine glasses— the same pattern that was used by the Granthams on the set of *Downton Abbey*. I'd had them shipped from England, and she absolutely loved them.

But the best gift was yet to come. She gave it to me later that morning when Scott was busy on the living room floor, assembling a new baby-bouncer for Louise from Barbara and George.

Bev shepherded me into the bathroom, shut the door, and withdrew a tiny gift bag from beneath her oversized blue sweatshirt. "This is an extra gift to you from me," she said. "It came by special overnight express delivery, direct from the North Pole."

I grinned at her with mischief. "Wow. I don't think I've ever had a special express delivery from the North Pole before. I can't wait to see what's inside."

I reached into the bag, removed the red tissue paper, and withdrew a pregnancy test.

"Where in the world did you get this?" I asked.

She raised an eyebrow. "I had to call in a favor last night. You didn't see me buckling Louise into the car and driving off, not long after we got home?"

"No," I replied with dismay. "Where did you go?"

She shrugged as if it were nothing. "There's a pharmacist in the city and she owed me a favor for looking after her kids for a weekend about a year ago. I told her about your situation. She's a really nice lady and she took good care of me."

I shook my head in disbelief and felt a lump form in my throat. "I love that there are still good people in the world."

Bev nodded. "Of course there are. Santa has plenty of helpers. So this is your special gift from the world to use at will, because I thought you might appreciate the chance to terminate the suspense as quickly as possible."

I began to gently shove Bev out of the bathroom. "You are an angel sent from heaven, and this is the perfect Christmas gift. With that said, I am sure you won't be offended if I ask you to leave so that I can pee on it."

Bev laughed and stepped out of the room.

Epilogue

One year later

"We're going to need a ladder to put the angel on top," I said to Scott as I reached into the box for the last few ornaments.

The living room was a disaster with boxes of decorations spread out everywhere and wrapped gifts piled on the dining room table, waiting to be displayed under the tree.

"A chair should do it," he said, moving to the dining room to get one.

Bev was feeding Louise in the high chair in the kitchen, while Leo gobbled up Cheerios as they fell from the tray onto the floor.

Our five-month old daughter, Serena, giggled and cooed as my mother carried her around the breakfast bar, bouncing at the knees.

Scott brought a dining room chair to the tree, and I passed him the angel to set on top. It wobbled for a few seconds until he found the right balance, then he plugged it into the string of white lights.

Getting down off the chair, he reached for my hand so

we could stand back and admire our tree together.

"It's beautiful," I said, wrapping my arms around his waist and resting my cheek on his chest.

Serena let out a happy shriek and we both turned to look her. My mother smiled at us. "It sounds like she likes it, too."

I left Scott to tidy up the boxes while I moved to take Serena from my mother's arms and carry her on my hip to examine the sparkly tree ornaments among the evergreen boughs. I was just fingering a gold trumpet on a string when the doorbell rang.

"I'll get it." Scott set down the empty boxes and moved to answer it.

"Good evening," he said to the uniformed courier who stood outside on our front step in the cold. "You're working late."

"There's always plenty of overtime when it gets this close to Christmas," he explained as he handed a package the size of a shoebox to Scott and asked him to sign for it.

A moment later, Scott closed the door and brought the box over to me. He stared down at the return address, hesitated briefly, then said, "It's for you."

Slightly unnerved by the look in his eye, I swapped Serena for the package. While he carried our daughter to the kitchen to join Bev, Louise, and my mother, I checked to see who it was from.

"It's from Angie," I said with a sudden spark of unease as I moved to the coffee table and sat down. My reaction wasn't rational of course. I had moved on a long time ago and had let go of any lingering animosity, but I suppose she would always be my late-husband's ex-lover and the friend who had betrayed me in the worst possible way. Seeing this package from her was an unexpected reminder.

The others were quiet while I ripped off the packing tape and opened the outer box. Inside, there was a card in a red envelope that said "Claire," along with a smaller gift wrapped in festive paper and shiny gold ribbon, all on a bed of green tissue paper.

The others watched quietly while I opened the card and began to read the letter.

Dear Claire,

It's been a long time since we've spoken, and I'm not sure how you will feel when you receive this package from me, but I felt a great need to make contact with you this holiday season.

First of all, congratulations on the birth of your daughter. Barbara let me know that everything went well, and I am very happy for you and Scott. No one deserves happiness more than the two of you.

As for me... I do not feel worthy of all the gifts you have sent my way over the past year, much less your kindness and forgiveness.

For that reason, I feel a deep and unrelenting need to thank you, and to let you know that you have made a tremendous difference in my life. Something changed in me when Barbara arrived with the Christmas gift that came from you, not long before I went into labor last year. She told me what you had said in your letter to her, and I was deeply, deeply humbled. But still, I couldn't bring myself to contact you, because I was too ashamed.

Then Wesley was born, and the love he brought with him when he came into the world exploded inside of me. I can't explain it, but his birth, coupled with your forgiveness, was a true miracle in my life. I never felt more blessed, and I knew in that moment that I would never again intentionally inflict pain on another human being, nor would I betray a friendship, or act without honor or integrity. I want to be a good example for my son and be the best person I can possibly be. All I have to do is think of you, and I have a shining example to emulate.

Thank you, Claire—not just for the money, which has been extremely helpful to me as a single mother—but for your selflessness and forgiveness, your loving nature, and for showing me how to be a better person.

Which brings us to this moment, a year later, approaching Christmas. Please find enclosed a gift for you and Scott, and you can probably guess what's inside.

Barbara and I decided together that you should have it, because it is a cup full of love, and no one deserves it more than you.

I feel certain that if Wes is looking down on all of us—which I believe he is—he would approve of my choice to pass this along to you. Please know that he was very sorry for the mistakes he made and the pain he caused you. His regret and shame weighed heavily on his heart.

So now, here we are. I will move forward with sadness over the loss of a man I loved and the friend I had not treated as she deserved to be treated. But I will endeavor to go on with joy for all the blessings I have received, and for the lessons I have learned. I will spend the rest of my days making myself worthy of those gifts.

Merry Christmas, Claire. May you always be surrounded by joy and love and Christmas miracles. You deserve that more than anyone.

Sincerely,

Angie

As I finished reading the letter, I wiped tears from my cheeks and found myself smiling.

I set it down on the coffee table and reached for the gift. Pulling the gold ribbon free, I opened the box and found the gleaming sterling silver baby cup and spoon that Barbara had given to me a few Christmases ago, when Wes and I were just beginning our journey together with the dream of creating a family.

So much had happened since then. There had been pain and heartbreak, but today there was nothing but an overflowing cup of joy and love.

I stood and turned to hold it up for Scott, Bev, and my mom to see. "It's from Angie," I said, my voice trembling with emotion. "She wrote me the most wonderful letter."

Scott immediately came to my side, where we stood among the mess gazing into each other's eyes, rejoicing and feeling grateful for all the little miracles that had brought us together.

And given us Serena.

My mother joined us as well. I handed her the letter to read.

She took a moment to get through it, then looked up at me with damp eyes.

"You did the right thing, Claire. Do you know how proud your father would be, if he were here with us today?"

I nodded as tears filled my eyes. "He *is* here, Mom." I touched my fist to my heart. "He's right in here, and he always will be."

Scott kissed me softly on the cheek, while our baby daughter reached for the cup with her clumsy little baby hands. We all laughed and returned to the task of decorating our home for Christmas, while the angel at the top of the tree shone her light brightly and smiled down upon us all.

Dear Reader,

Thank you for taking the time to read *The Color of a Christmas Miracle*. I hope it provided you with a few hours of reading pleasure and touched your heart in some way.

If this is your first time reading one of the books in my *Color of Heaven* series, I encourage you to start at the beginning with *The Color of Heaven*, and work your way through the books in order. You can find the series order on my website book page at www.juliannemaclean.com.

And I hope you will also look for Bev's story, coming in June 2017. In *The Color of a Silver Lining*, Bev will confront the choices she has made as a single mother raising her child alone, and as often happens in this series, the magic of the universe will conspire to lead her in the direction she is meant to go. The ebook is available for pre-order now at all major online retailers.

If you would like to stay informed about that book and other novels I'm working on, please sign up for my newsletter so that I can send you an email. I would love to send news to you.

And if you would like to know when any of my backlist titles go on sale for 99 cents or are offered for free for a limited time, please follow me on Bookbub so that you won't miss out on these deals.

I also encourage you to enter the monthly giveaway on my website, where I send an autographed print edition from my extensive backlist to one lucky winner each month.

That's all for now. Best wishes and happy reading!
Julianne

OTHER BOOKS IN THE

COLOR OF HEAVEN SERIES

The COLOR *of* HEAVEN

Book One

A deeply emotional tale about Sophie Duncan, a successful columnist whose world falls apart after her daughter's unexpected illness and her husband's shocking affair. When it seems nothing else could possibly go wrong, her car skids off an icy road and plunges into a frozen lake. There, in the cold dark depths of the water, a profound and extraordinary experience unlocks the surprising secrets from Sophie's past, and teaches her what it means to truly live…and love.

Full of surprising twists and turns and a near-death experience that will leave you breathless, this story is not to be missed.

"A gripping, emotional tale you'll want to read in one sitting."
—*New York Times* bestselling author, Julia London

"Brilliantly poignant mainstream tale."
—4 ½ starred review, *Romantic Times*

Includes Bonus Content: A Bookclub Discussion Guide

The COLOR *of* DESTINY

Book Two

Eighteen years ago a teenage pregnancy changed Kate Worthington's life forever. Faced with many difficult decisions, she chose to follow her heart and embrace an uncertain future with the father of her baby—her devoted first love.

At the same time, in another part of the world, sixteen-year-old Ryan Hamilton makes his own share of mistakes, but learns important lessons along the way. Twenty years later, Kate's and Ryan's paths cross in a way they could never expect, which makes them question the possibility of destiny. Even when all seems hopeless, could it be that everything happens for a reason, and we end up exactly where we are meant to be?

Includes Bonus Content: A Bookclub Discussion Guide

The COLOR *of* HOPE

Book Three

Diana Moore has led a charmed life. She is the daughter of a wealthy senator and lives a glamorous city life, confident that her handsome live-in boyfriend Rick is about to propose. But everything is turned upside down when she learns of a mysterious woman who works nearby—a woman who is her identical mirror image.

Diana is compelled to discover the truth about this woman's identity, but the truth leads her down a path of secrets, betrayals, and shocking discoveries about her past. These discoveries follow her like a shadow.

Then she meets Dr. Jacob Peterson—a brilliant cardiac surgeon with an uncanny ability to heal those who are broken. With his help, Diana embarks upon a journey to restore her belief in the human spirit, and recover a sense of hope—that happiness, and love, may still be within reach for those willing to believe in second chances.

Includes Bonus Content: A Bookclub Discussion Guide

The COLOR *of*
A DREAM

Book Four

Nadia Carmichael has had a lifelong run of bad luck. It begins on the day she is born, when she is separated from her identical twin sister and put up for adoption. Twenty-seven years later, not long after she is finally reunited with her twin and is expecting her first child, Nadia falls victim to a mysterious virus and requires a heart transplant.

Now recovering from the surgery with a new heart, Nadia is haunted by a recurring dream that sets her on a path to discover the identity of her donor. Her efforts are thwarted, however, when the father of her baby returns to sue for custody of their child. It's not until Nadia learns of his estranged brother Jesse that she begins to explore the true nature of her dreams, and discover what her new heart truly needs and desires…

The COLOR *of* A MEMORY

Book Five

Audrey Fitzgerald believed she was married to the perfect man—a heroic firefighter who saved lives, even beyond his own death. But a year later she meets a mysterious woman who has some unexplained connection to her husband...

Soon Audrey discovers that her husband was keeping secrets and she is compelled to dig into his past. Little does she know...this journey of self-discovery will lead her down a path to a new and different future—a future she never could have imagined.

The COLOR *of* LOVE

Book Six

Carla Matthews is a single mother struggling to make ends meet and give her daughter Kaleigh a decent upbringing. When Kaleigh's absent father Seth—a famous alpine climber who never wanted to be tied down—begs for a second chance at fatherhood, Carla is hesitant because she doesn't want to pin her hopes on a man who is always seeking another mountain to scale. A man who was never willing to stay put in one place and raise a family.

But when Seth's plane goes missing after a crash landing in the harsh Canadian wilderness, Carla must wait for news… Is he dead or alive? Will the wreckage ever be found?

One year later, after having given up all hope, Carla receives a phone call that shocks her to her core. A man has been found, half-dead, floating on an iceberg in the North Atlantic, uttering her name. Is this Seth? And is it possible that he will come home to her and Kaleigh at last, and be the man she always dreamed he would be?

Includes Bonus Content: A Bookclub Discussion Guide

The COLOR *of*
THE SEASON

Book Seven

From *USA Today* bestselling author Julianne MacLean comes the next installment in her popular Color of Heaven series—a gripping, emotional tale about real life magic that touches us all during the holiday season...

Boston cop, Josh Wallace, is having the worst day of his life. First, he's dumped by the woman he was about to propose to, then everything goes downhill from there when he is shot in the line of duty. While recovering in the hospital, he can't seem to forget the woman he wanted to marry, nor can he make sense of the vivid images that flashed before his eyes when he was wounded on the job. Soon, everything he once believed about his life begins to shift when he meets Leah James, an enigmatic resident doctor who somehow holds the key to both his past and his future...

The COLOR *of* JOY

Book Eight

After rushing to the hospital for the birth of their third child, Riley and Lois James anticipate one of the most joyful days of their lives. But things take a dark turn when their newborn daughter vanishes from the hospital. Is this payback for something in Riley's troubled past? Or is it something even more mysterious?

As the search intensifies and the police close in, strange and unbelievable clues about the whereabouts of the newborn begin to emerge, and Riley soon finds himself at the center of a surprising turn of events that will challenge everything he once believed about life, love, and the existence of miracles.

The COLOR *of* TIME

Book Nine

They say it's impossible to change the past...

Since her magical summer romance at the age of sixteen, Sylvie Nichols has never been able to forget her first love.

Years later, when she returns to the seaside town where she lost her heart to Ethan Foster, she is determined to lay the past to rest once and for all. But letting go becomes a challenge when Sylvie finds herself transported back to that long ago summer of love...and the turbulent events that followed. Soon, past and present begin to collide in strange and mystifying ways, and Sylvie can't help but wonder if a true belief in miracles is powerful enough to change both her past and her future....

The COLOR *of* FOREVER

Book Ten

Recently divorced television reporter Katelyn Roberts has stopped believing in relationships that last forever, until a near-death experience during a cycling accident changes everything. When she miraculously survives unscathed, a long-buried mystery leads her to the quaint, seaside town of Cape Elizabeth, Maine.

There, on the rugged, windswept coast of the Atlantic, she finds herself caught up in the secrets of a historic inn that somehow calls to her from the past. Is it possible that the key to her true destiny lies beneath all that she knows, as she explores the grand mansion and property? Or that the great love she's always dreamed of is hidden in the alcoves of its past?

The COLOR *of* A PROMISE

Book Eleven

Having spent a lifetime in competition with his older brother Aaron—who always seemed to get the girl—Jack Peterson leaves the U.S. to become a foreign correspondent in the Middle East. When a roadside bomb forces him to return home to recover from his wounds, he quickly becomes the most celebrated journalist on television, and is awarded his own prime time news program. Now, wealthy and successful beyond his wildest dreams, Jack believes he has finally found where he is meant to be. But when a 747 explodes in the sky over his summer house in Cape Elizabeth, all hell breaks loose as the wreckage crashes to the ground. He has no idea that his life is about to take another astonishing turn…

Meg Andrews grew up with a fear of flying, but when it meant she wouldn't be able to visit her boyfriend on the opposite side of the country, she confronted her fear head-on and earned her pilot's license. Now, a decade later, she is a respected airline crash investigator, passionate about her work, to the point of obsession. When she arrives in the picturesque seaside community of Cape Elizabeth to investigate a massive airline disaster, she meets the famous and charismatic Jack Peterson, who has his own personal fascination with plane crashes.

As the investigation intensifies, Meg and Jack feel a powerful, inexplicable connection to each other. Soon, they realize that the truth behind the crash—and the mystery of their connection—can only be discovered through the strength of the human spirit, the timeless bonds of family, and the gift of second chances.

Coming in June 2017

The COLOR
of a
SILVER LINING

"It makes the reader think about what could have been, and loves past, and makes you wonder if you are leading the life you're meant to be leading. Thought-provoking, emotionally-intense and riveting, Ms. MacLean delivers another 5-star romance in The Color of Forever."

—Nancy at Goodreads

"Wow! The Color of Heaven was intriguing, emotional, heartbreaking, inspiring, breathtaking, and touched me very profoundly. You will not be able to put it down but I encourage you to absorb the depth of the characters and their journeys. Thank you!!"

—Amazon reviewer

"Spell Binding! My first read by Julianne…wow, I am hooked! I couldn't stop reading this intriguing story. Look forward to the next one."

—Iris at Amazon

"Emotionally moving! There are many twists, some predictable, some not. Heartfelt!"

—GEA at Amazon

"Loved it!"   —Christa at Amazon

"Fabulous read. I thoroughly enjoyed this book. Well written. Lots of interesting subjects covered. Characters lovely and rich. A worthwhile read! Looking forward to sampling the next book in the series."

—Sandra at Amazon

"Heavenly book!"   —Bobbi at Amazon

About the Author

Julianne MacLean is a *USA Today* bestselling author of many historical romances, including The Highlander Series with St. Martin's Press and her popular American Heiress Series with Avon/Harper Collins. She also writes contemporary mainstream fiction, and The Color of Heaven was a *USA Today* bestseller. She is a three-time RITA finalist, and has won numerous awards, including the Booksellers' Best Award, the Book Buyer's Best Award, and a Reviewers' Choice Award from Romantic Times for Best Regency Historical of 2005. She lives in Nova Scotia with her husband and daughter, and is a dedicated member of Romance Writers of Atlantic Canada. Please visit Julianne's website for more information and to subscribe to her mailing list to stay informed about upcoming releases.

www.juliannemaclean.com

OTHER BOOKS BY

JULIANNE MACLEAN

The American Heiress Series

To Marry the Duke
An Affair Most Wicked
My Own Private Hero
Love According to Lily
Portrait of a Lover
Surrender to a Scoundrel

The Pembroke Palace Series

In My Wildest Fantasies
The Mistress Diaries
When a Stranger Loves Me
Married By Midnight
A Kiss Before the Wedding – A Pembroke Palace Short Story
Seduced at Sunset

The Highlander Trilogy

The Rebel – A Highland Short Story
Captured by the Highlander
Claimed by the Highlander
Seduced by the Highlander
Return of the Highlander
Taken by the Highlander

The Royal Trilogy

Be My Prince
Princess in Love
The Prince's Bride

Dodge City Brides Trilogy

Mail Order Prairie Bride
Tempting the Marshal
Taken by the Cowboy – a Time Travel Romance

Colonial Romance

Adam's Promise

Contemporary Fiction

The Color of Heaven
The Color of Destiny
The Color of Hope
The Color of a Dream
The Color of a Memory
The Color of Love
The Color of the Season
The Color of Joy
The Color of Time
The Color of Forever
The Color of a Promise
The Color of a Christmas Miracle
The Color of a Silver Lining

Made in the USA
Columbia, SC
12 July 2022

63384384R00143